WHAT HAPPENED TO US

WHAT HAPPENED TO US

FICTIONS

A Novel
by Ian Holding

LITTLE ISLAND PRESS

Lodgemore Lane,
Stroud, GL5 3EQ

Published in the United Kingdom by
Little Island Press, Stroud

First Published 2018

ISBN 978-1-9998549-0-4

Series design by t.r.u
typographic research unit

Typeset in Bembo MT
Printed and bound in Great Britain by TJ International

CONTENTS

WHAT HAPPENED TO US

1

I THINK WHAT HAPPENED TO US started the day I was out playing on the streets of our neighbourhood and accidently pissed on the President's face. I was a thirteen year old kid, skinny, lean-boned, full of shit. It was a Tuesday afternoon and I was home early from school on a scorching early November day. There hadn't been any rainfall yet to ease the tight, dry heat or settle the dust, and I was out and about amongst it, blood-hot, looking for trouble.

This small convenience shop sat at the edge of a circular field. It was more of a bottle store, at the end of a row of three shop buildings, and it was run down, a bit grubby. We never used it unless Mom ran short of milk or sugar so she'd send Petra down to see if they had any in stock, but it was popular with the domestic workers from around the neighbourhood. Dad said it had become a bit of a *shabeen* and I shouldn't hang out there, but that only added to its allure. Sometimes at weekends, at dusk on a Sunday, there was twangy gospel music blaring from a blown speaker, and the mob of people on the *stoep* jigged about in an aura of sweet-smelling smoke.

During the weekdays it was calm, sedate, low-key. Flat red soil ran along the wide ground in front of it, scattered with small gritty stones, dry tufts of lime-white grass. Upturned fruit slats balanced on bricks had items for sale spread across them, tomatoes, cabbages, charred mealies on the cob. A row of grim nannies oversaw it, their fat arses sat on small stools, looking generally annoyed with life. They were my victims, my play things for the afternoon as I glided in, owning a straggled line of them in my crazed vision.

The first thing I did was race the narrow corridor behind them, between their line of stalls and the cracked concrete *stoep* of the shops, before braking hard, leaning in and turning my handle bars down at an angle I could just control. The effect was great, soil swelling in my wake, rising in a cloud, smoking everyone with a rusty layer of fine dust.

'*Mufana*,' they said. 'Hey, hey, you go away, go away.'

I called back, loud and mocking.

This was taken as a threat. One was up and after me, lumbering through the collapsing sheets of dust, her dark arms flapping, her screen-printed T-shirt barely containing her massive boobs and the rest of her bulk wrapped in a skirt of loud zig-zag print fabric. It was those jagged strokes I saw staggering towards me that made me think I was deep to the neck in the crap this time.

But I was too fast. Swift and energised. I was up on my haunches, kicking down at my pedals, cruising the cusp of the crescent in no time, yards and walls and gates streaming soundlessly by, and I'd left her shaking her fists at me, yelling at me in Shona to stay away. This was only a challenge for round two, a second assault. I circled back, laughing my head off.

THIS USUALLY CARRIED ON until I grew tired. There were only so many nannies you could rag and run away from before your legs got stiff, a thirst dried out your throat. Plus on this particular day I needed a short rest and a quick piss. I pedalled round the back of the bottle store, lent the bike against the brickwork and took a slash against the wall, sure this tall flange of dry bush acted as a bit of a screen.

It was only when I was shaking dry I realised the entire rear wall of the bottle store had been strung up with these glossy banners in yellow, green and black stripes and they had writing on them, quotes and slogans around this centre

14

picture, and in fact I had been busy sloshing a firm jet of pee at a supersized image of a pair of square glasses, behind which were two distinctive dark eyes, opal black, a rim of red round the pupils, both cased in a stark off-white slip. It was the President's face. Oh shit. Not good at all. I felt this immediate lung-drained panic of having done something very wrong, very bad. I quickly pulled back and hopped on the bike, racing off round the front again. I didn't think anyone saw me, it didn't feel as if anyone did, but you never can be sure.

For several seconds I kept expecting an angry swarming mob to come charging after me, but no one did. I decided to play it cool, to hang around for a bit, launch a fresh attack as if nothing had happened. I swooped through the passage again before curving off, breaking and grazing my tyres across the loose red soil. Again the sheets of dust furled. But even the nannies had given up chasing me now, resigned to the heat and their quiet fury at this cheeky white boy. Their shouting and cussing, threatening to march off to call a cop, send the war vet militias after me, all came to nothing and they knew it as well as I did that this was their bitch bad lot of a stinking hot afternoon. In the leafy northern suburbs the white kid was king.

In a way I was disappointed my antics hadn't caused more of a stir. It was a flat anti-climax. I craved the high drama of inciting the locals, longing for their animated histrionics to serve as a counterpoint to my own tame suburban background. It had the promise of being thrillingly entertaining. At the same time an older part of me knew this brand of shit-stirring was bordering on becoming distasteful anyway, a touch pathetic.

I pulled away from the grime and the groans and started to make my way up Alice Smith road, slugging hard at the pedals as I began to climb the hill. Sweat sluiced my baked brow, the nearly hairless hollow of my armpits. I rocked on the bike to build a rhythm but my legs gave in, failing me three-quarters the way up. I stopped, panting. I slid off the saddle and began to wheel the bike next to me. It was hot as hell.

I NOTICED THREE MEN slink into focus behind me. Two were tall, lanky, swaggering. The third was shorter, stockier, strolling with a smug rocking movement as if wired into some hip inner vibe. They wore blue workman's overalls, the same bog-standard design you saw everywhere about town. They might have been working somewhere in the neighbourhood, installers, contractors or craftsmen, but to me they were just this formless trio loping over my shoulder, an irregular moving mass. They had been at the bottle store, carrying scuds of *chibuku* in boxed blue and white tubular cartons which they raised to their lips, then steadied with both hands as they drank. Had they seen me pissing on the President? Were they coming after me? I kept thinking I was going to be clapped to hell and dumped in a ditch. When I glanced back, I caught the rhubarb-dark eye of the shorter man and a silent, intense scorn narrowed in towards me. They were getting closer, faster than I was, lazy and spent, pushing a bike up the nape of a hill. They were closing in on me all the time.

I wouldn't let them pass me. A tug deep within told me I couldn't, not once I had met that pair of stark angry eyes. I needed to get away. The hot silence between us told me very clearly. When they were just a few feet behind me and I could almost feel their hot beer breaths on the back of my neck, I reached the summit of the hill and in a flash was on my bike again gliding down with glorious triumph, freewheeling at a speed that was so foolhardy a gangly wobble crept into my front tyre. I was home now, with some relief. I applied pressure to the brakes as I arched into our driveway, No. 11 Alice Smith Road.

MY ARRIVAL DISTURBED SOMETHING. There was a moving lump in the thick shrub beside the wall and a strange new fright overcame me as I stared wide-eyed into all that mottled darkness. Something was about to jump out, pounce on me. But deep in the olive brown I traced the outline of a ginger cat, a stray crouched down, its sharp ears erect at my arrival. I considered flushing it from its den, chasing it, but it had already outthought me and was scaling the wall, sliding its fat belly over the ledge into our garden where it cantered away in a heartbeat.

'Frickin cat,' I said.

I slipped the blue and grey oval-shaped remote from my pocket, pressed the red button. The gate coasted back on its rollers and I stepped into the yard but before I closed it, I glanced back at the blurred shape of those three men sauntering down the lip of the hill.

DESPITE BEING IN A ROLLING, up-and-down kind of suburb, our yard is wide and flat and once inside its walls the distance to the road affords a sense of isolation. Yet no sooner had I stashed my bike against the side of the garage, stripped to my briefs and chucked myself into the glorious relief of the pool, I heard the gate bell. It bellowed out from the house, its sharp pitched ring jutting across the tight ripples of the pool towards my half-submerged face, my ears conch-like and alert, aware this energy originated from the road where I'd just been.

There was no one home except Petra and Ignatius. It was

Tuesday so Petra was out in the laundry room labouring over the ironing board. Mom always complained that she never heard what her stubborn old *ambuya* ears didn't want to. Ignatius was nowhere to be seen either, the garden just broad and motionless, as if flattened by heat. Even the dogs were out of action, splayed on the cool slatestone of the veranda.

All this inertia seemed to heighten the sound of the gate bell ringing from the house. I treaded the water beneath me, stilling myself, listening, figuring that the area around me was probably amplifying the sound. We were taught this at school and I suddenly couldn't bear to think that the noise of the gate bell might travel towards me again, a slingshot skimming a flat surface. If it did I knew whoever was on the other side of the gate was calling for me, and no one would come to my defence. Faint guilt chilled through me, my skin tightened in the water.

I waited, tensed, eyes widened, my legs treading silently beneath me. A stinging rush of chlorine rifled up my nose, but there was no sound beyond the gentle lapping of the water against the curvy rim of the pool. I sneezed violently, a volley of slobbered snot jellying the water.

'Oh gross,' I said, feeling the need to kill the tension.

LATER MOM AND DAD WERE HOME. It was around four-thirty. We were all on the wide veranda overlooking the pool. Mom made tea but Dad had an ice-cold beer. Mom had tea despite the heat and I had tea too, but with lots of milk, and fresh butter cookies Petra baked earlier in the day. They crumbled when you ate them and Mom sometimes complained about that, but I liked them.

'Danny enough now,' Mom said, after I scoffed three in quick succession.

The garden was as dry as the Sahara and Ignatius was fighting a losing battle standing in his blue overalls and black mud-shat gumboots, hosepipe in hand, water limply tumbling out the spout, scattering loose crystalline arcs across the scrawny flowerbeds. Even from the veranda I could sense the cracked, webby, light-red soil soften and darken, ooze under the flow of water, that wonderful rich scent of damp earth filling the air. I breathed it in deeply, cooling my lungs, loving how it left the faintest metallic aftertaste, a sprinkling of iron deep from the bowels of the earth.

'I don't know why he bothers,' Dad said, lazily. 'This bloody heat.'

'I hope we're not in for a drought,' Mom said.

'Well apparently, according to the papers, the powers that be have already declared there's another drought on the way.'

'Now there's a big surprise,' Mom said as she glanced over at Ignatius inching closer towards the veranda one desperate dying flowerbed at a time. She looked irritated. 'I don't know why he always has to make a sudden miraculous appearance just as we come out to have arvie tea.'

'Hey,' said Dad, whistling sharply, 'go around the back. Go water there. In fact go wash the car.'

'Yes boss.'

Ignatius coiled up the thick hose behind him and tramped out of sight.

'How many bloody droughts have we supposedly had in the last twelve years ever since the farmers were booted off?' Dad said.

'I suppose that's a rhetorical question,' Mom replied with a faint hint of bitterness.

'*Muntuland!*' Dad said, shrugging. 'Nothing ever bloody changes from year to year. You'd think they'd had enough of stuffing everything up. Have you seen the papers today?'

'What's in them?' Mom asked after a short pause. Dad shook his head, blowing air into his cheeks. Then he exhaled.

'No, it's just this bloody indigenisation issue. They're ratcheting up the big deal talk of taking over the businesses again.'

'It's probably all hot air,' Mom said. 'Don't even get worked up about it again. Not after all the palaver we went through last time only to have it all peter out.'

'I don't know. It seems they're intent. Even gazetted a new compliance deadline. It's all part of the election hysteria. Something to sprout to the masses about, their so-called economically deprived, colonially disadvantaged, whatever they like to call it from one week to the next. You know how they work. Same with the farms.'

'Let's not worry about it now,' Mom said.

'Yeah, we'll see. Trick is to get ahead of it all before they really clamp down, shift the goal posts yet again.'

'You never know whether you're Arthur or Martha in this place.'

'Anyway I'm working on a plan,' Dad said.

'Oh?'

'Yeah. We'll see, but it has to be done, sooner or later.'

'Hey Mom,' I said, sitting forward in the wicker chair.

'Yes Danny.'

'What's a rhetorical question?'

A SHORT WHILE LATER I heard Dad's stern voice round the front of the house, telling Ignatius off. There was no mistaking it, I could tell from the crude simple language and a totally abandoned caution he was putting Ignatius firmly in his place. Mom and I exchanged a short glance, neither approving nor disapproving, and Mom carried on thumbing through the latest edition of *YOU Magazine*, while I sauntered round the edge of the veranda, then the front of the house where the garages and bricked driveway came into view. Dad was standing by the side of his silver Toyota Hilux V-100 twin-cab, beer in hand, pointing down to an area on the side of the driver's door. Ignatius was down on his knees, rubbing at the shiny pewter greyness, nodding at Dad's instructions. Dad pointed to another area, this time on the bonnet.

'Here,' he said. 'No, gently, like this.'

He mimicked the circular motion of the polishing action and Ignatius again nodded, eager to obey. I looked at the impressive figure of the muscular Hilux, shimmering in the late afternoon sun and the thought of its gruff roar fuelled pleasure in me. I was thinking of one of those car adverts on TV, the rugged outdoor life, health, vitality, family, the bounding shaggy dog, unpoliced speed, sunshine eternal, emerald green hills and an upbeat soundtrack which said everything was right with the world. Dad had bought into the Toyota Hilux ideal of that life for us too, if only the bloody government hoods wouldn't steal all our tax bucks from the country's coffers, he said, make the whole place destitute.

I went back to the veranda. He came through the house a few minutes later.

'I've just given that bloody Ignatius a blast,' he said.

'Why now?' Mom asked.

'Doesn't listen to instructions. Uses the dirty rags to polish with instead of the roll of new mutton-cloth. I keep telling him all he's doing is spreading the dirt around, but do you think I can get him to realise that?'

'You have to tell him things repeatedly, make it clear,' she said. 'Remember his English isn't all that great.'

Dad didn't respond but he looked mildly incensed at something more offensive than a mere oily smudge on the side of his pride-and-joy car.

BEING HOME FOR ONCE IN THE AFTERNOON, or due to the oozy elastic nature of the heat, the day was stretching more aimlessly than most. When Mom trailed through to the kitchen at around five to oversee preparations for dinner, and Dad followed her to fish another beer from the freezer, I took the opportunity to slip off the veranda and sneak to the boundary of our property where I quietly climbed up the spindly trunk of the coffee shade tree. It forked out into our neighbour's yard, our old friends the Whitakers. The grey rough-cast concrete wall separating us was no more than two metres high and this quick shimmy up the branches gave me a clear-sighted view of their prefab garages across the bank of a shrub-dotted rockery, some dry lawn, a tar-laid driveway. I could see that both lazy-man doors of their garage were open, no cars visible. It was a sneaky way of telling whether Amy was home from school yet, making me seem less keen in the process, more chilled than having to message her to find out. I did a quick mental check. Tuesday. Probably had flute band practice. It didn't usually end until after dark. That explained it.

WHEN I JUMPED OFF THE TREE and peeled myself out of the bushes to come back to the veranda, I saw that Dad hadn't returned from the kitchen. He never lingered in that domain very long, not with Mom and Petra fussing over dinner. Because I'd normally only be back from school around this time, we'd usually have a few minutes by ourselves, 'just the boys' as Mom called us. He'd ask me about school and sport and because I was beat I'd always just say it was fine, or okay. He was also tired too after a long day at work so this satisfied him, his duty seen to. Then we'd talk a bit of harmless horse-crap or play chess or cards or sometimes French cricket on the lawn with the dogs if either of us had energy. In winter we'd be in doors and then it was an easy excuse not to talk but to turn the TV on, watch the day's sports highlights on the sports catch-up channel.

I took a few steps into the lounge, then up the passage to see if I could gauge his whereabouts. A part of me hoped he was just on the loo, or checking emails on the family computer. I was disconcerted about his mood, that he was more than usually uptight, weighed down with all these hassles which hadn't slipped off him nearly as quickly as they normally did once he was home and relaxing with a beer, the family, the dogs.

He wasn't in the loo but in the kitchen. I could hear him there, talking to Mom. As I hovered in the passage I could only see through to the figure of Petra in her pale blue and small pink-flowered maid's outfit standing by the sink in the scullery with a peeler in her hands and a colander of potatoes. She seemed detached from the low-grade intensity of the drama that was airing just a few feet away from her, but I could detect it in an instant.

They were continuing their earlier discussion about the situation with the company, talking quietly, in low deadpan voices, some distaste in what they were saying. I wasn't interested in all this business and politics crap, the various ramifications of it. I just caught something disarming in their hardened, angular way of speaking, almost a kind of flat despondency, a weakened resolve, and then

23

the gravelled uneasy mood that followed it out into the passageway where I'd stood, snooping on them. I moved off to my bedroom but it was something I couldn't easily shake off.

Sitting for a few moments on the end of my bed, I was oddly nervous, remnants of that quick panic from earlier in the afternoon. I wondered whether I had crossed a line this time, breached a tipping point, and if the uneasy begrudging peace we always lived with had now been somehow threatened. But it was my failure to define or understand these bigger consequences, and how to draw the lines between the dots, that really confounded me. I was always just aware of this vague, brooding fragility around everything we said and did, the way we lived even. A short but intense feeling of non-specific guilt clouded in on me, just lasting a few seconds, a cold shudder from within.

I SHRUGGED IT OFF as an overreaction, a hot muddle. I was sure no one had seen me round the back of the bottle store anyway. I was certain if they had it would've provoked an instant backlash, especially in the fiery environment of an election season where tensions were stacked about like bundles of dry tinder. It was just a mistake, it could be explained, surely? Of course it could. I scooped up my cell phone from a small pine desk and absently punched in my pin number. There was only one Facebook notification, a stupid clip one of my friends had posted of some drunk guy slipping off the end of a diving board and smacking onto the concrete surrounds of a pool while all around his rowdy pals howled with laughter, beer cans in hand. It was lame, I hardly even chuckled. Then there was a message posted to the WhatsApp group I belonged to called 'CRICKET XI'. 'Check this wicked shit out,' the message said from one of the guys. A video clip followed which I clicked on to begin downloading more as a matter of habit than urgent desire. The circle started spinning, then moved slowly clockwise. My expectations were entirely dispassionate by now, but I played it all the same. It was a ten second clip of an averagely hot naked woman with impressive boobs, long ashen-streaked blonde hair, looking and pouting seductively at the camera, deep in the throes of pleasure while rubbing a large white oiled dildo against the folds of her moistened, shaven vagina. I made sure to have the speakers on my phone turned off, but by the tunnelled sucking movements of her mouth she was obviously making the appropriate groaning and moaning noises. The clip didn't do anything to excite me, not then, but I replied with a thumps-up sign anyway to signal my cool approval. I put my phone face down again on my desk and went out of my stuffy room to see if I could salvage anything of the open air.

NOT EVEN BY SIX was the temperature falling. The blazing sun dimmed slightly at an angle in the domed glass blue sky and eventually began to mellow to a fierce, melting red. When the light finally fell it went quickly enough, leaving just this hot levitation of air. There were no insects. Not even mosquitoes. The dogs were cooling the underbelly of their necks on the veranda tiles where we had all congregated again.

There was no talk of business or politics now and that was a relief. The topic seemed to have slid away, though I keep observing Dad, with the impression he was deep in thought, leaving his outer features entirely blank. Mom encouraged him to go for a dip with her and afterwards he seemed different, fresher, calmer. Mom sat in her cozie with a light gauzy blue and silver screen-printed wrap pinned round her midriff. She nursed her glass of chilled white wine with oversized stubs of ice. Dad had his swim trunks on now, old faded black boxer shorts and he sat bare chested and I sat bare chested next to him while he helped me with my maths homework, sipping at the long iced neck of a frothy beer bottle. We snacked on raisins, salted peanuts.

'No, remember the long division rules,' Dad said. 'Come, try again.'

'Oh right,' I said, rubbing out my mistake with the inverted end of a pencil.

Mom got up, had a turn around the pool, the dogs trailing behind her, their tongues slackened, these flighty pink scarfs trailing from their slobbery mouths. She commented from afar on the pool needing a double dose of chlorine.

'It's this damn heat,' she said, 'zaps the chlorine from the pool in no time.'

Dad and I weren't really listening to her as she walked through to the kitchen to check on dinner.

'Let's eat out here, love,' Dad called after her.

MY SISTER, BECCA, finally arrived home from her dance class just as the last of the dusk light finally dissolved into night. It was nearing seven, the darkness moping just beyond the spread of outside lights. Mom had left the front door open for Becca since six, knowing she was always loaded down with a store of bags after a day's slog at school, then an evening of dance.

'Be nice and go and help your sister,' Mom said to me, patting me on the shoulder, edging me forward off the couch where I had migrated to watch *Two and a Half Men*.

'Mom, I'm watching.'

'Danny, be a gentleman,' she said.

I traipsed out the front door and turned towards the garages where she had parked her little strawberry-pink Fiat Uno. She was bent over, pooling bags from the boot. She was tired, I could see the heaviness and heat of the day slant right through her supple dancer's body, weighing down her slight shoulders. I ran over, scooped up the outline of a satchel from the tarmac. It weighed a tonne, stoned down with thick text books the likes of which, soon to be strewn over the dining room table until midnight, always sent something of a dreadful shiver through me. I didn't want to grow up, face the grind of all that.

'Hi Beccs,' I said.

'Hi Danny. Thanks a mil.'

I took another two bags, leaving only her dance kit bag, the one I knew was the lightest, and her cream-white school blazer she draped over her shoulder on a hanger. Weighed down like a bellhop I trudged towards the front door.

'Sorry Mom,' she said, 'we ending up reworking a whole routine from scratch.'

'Not to worry, love.'

No sooner had Becca walked in the front door, the power went off. It came as no surprise, but still the sudden plummet into darkness was always followed by a sharp collective Walker family exclamation, not so much because of the inconvenience of it, but as our own way of mocking the general state of affairs, as if to say, *Well done bloody government, you can't even keep the bloody lights on!*

'Danny, your turn,' Dad called.

I USED THE TORCH we hung up on a hook in the kitchen, flicked off the geyser switch on the DCB board in the scullery, then rotated the turn-over lever to the label marked GENNY. I went out into the courtyard where the 5.5 KVA yellow-and-black Kipor generator sat boxed under a makeshift plywood awning. I turned the key in the ignition and waited to hear the cylinders begin to clank into action as the diesel engine started up, immediately billowing gusts of thick black smoke out the spiral of its exhaust. I let it settle down to a purr and then flicked the switch on the amp gauge. Immediately the engine dipped under the strain of the load. The house lit up.

WE ATE ON OUR LAPS on the veranda. Within five minutes of Becca's return here we were, our family, supping away. I was famished, shovelling crumbed pork fillet, mash, carrots and beans nicely juiced in thick gravy.

'Crikey Dan, no one's going to take it away from you,' Mom said.

'Eat properly,' Dad added.

I slowed down a bit, feeling scorned and embarrassed.

Becca picked at hers.

'Not much of an appetite,' she said, grimacing and patting her flat stone-like belly.

'Me too,' Mom said. 'This heat.'

Then the gate bell rang. I froze, my fork midway to my mouth. I had almost been expecting this to happen, at least I felt this the second it sounded.

'Who the hell could that be?' Dad said, getting up.

He went through to the hallway, lifted the receiver.

'Hello,' he said. 'Hello.'

Outside we were semi-frozen. It was the odd timing of the whole thing that instantly threw up this edgy, fraught possibility. Had there been an accident out on the road? Had something happened? Then again, there was the dreadful hope hovering between us that this wasn't just a dull anti-climax either, a false alarm, someone off the streets asking for one of the servants or as they usually did in the afternoons, begging for food, for money.

'Hello,' Dad said again.

He came back outside, picked up his plate, sat down.

'Who was it?' Mom asked.

He shrugged. 'Dunno. No answer.'

A brief, hard bewildered glance ricocheted off us all, but in an instant it dissipated, and then the whole incident felt like nothing at all.

'Why was the front door left wide open?' Dad asked.

'Oh sorry,' said Becca, 'that was me.'

We carried on eating.

IT HAPPENED ONE MORE TIME that night. An hour or so later. Becca was lumped over the dining room table, headphones on, doing her homework. Mom and Dad had finally moved inside, though the French doors from the lounge to the veranda remained open, our only passage of respite. They had the overhead fan on turned up to max but all it did was whoop the stale air in laboured revolutions, churning the heat a couple of feet about the room. And at that speed it made a din, rattling so much that I couldn't really make out what the hell was happening on *CSI Miami*.

'I know, I know, my boy,' Dad said, 'it's bloody annoying. We'll have to see if we can fix it this weekend, okay, but until then it's better than nothing.'

Mom was fanning herself with a magazine, her legs up on the tan and white calf-skin foot stool.

'Danny,' she said, 'do us a favour love and take the ice cream out the freezer.'

I scooted up and dashed into the kitchen. The tub was wedged solid in a thick block of white frosted ice. Mom had all the fridges and freezers turned up full throttle.

Almost everything was iced over, even the milk, but it was safer this way she said. I pulled a knife from the knife set and began to hack away, instantly loving the muted tinny sound of the blade stabbing at the chinks that splintered off, shooting onto my hand, up my arm, beginning to dissolve almost at once against my warm flesh. Finally the tub broke free and the moment it did the gate bell sounded again. I stood still, tub outstretched before me, the freezer door ajar, spilling flows of silvered mist.

General exaggerated sighs were issued from the lounge. Not again, they were thinking. Once an evening was fraught with tingling possibility, twice was just a plain nuisance.

BUT IT WAS NOT TO ME. This was the third time for me now. Three suddenly became this suspicious, dangerous number.

'Danny, you're closest,' Mom shouted, 'please just see who that is.'

'Okay,' I said.

I walked stiffly to the intercom, pacing myself, though I still reached it from the kitchen, across the passage, in just a few shallow steps. I picked up the white receiver, placed it to my ear. A loud static thrum buzzed out, a currency of sound ushered from the roadside, though it seemed from another world altogether. All that separated us was a solid wall, a solid gate and a horrid feeling pitted in me of sensing someone there, stooping down to the speaker, breathing soundlessly close by it, or else even a small cluster of individuals gathered round the intercom post hushing themselves, listening for me as I listened for them. I was not going to say a word. I heard a soft metallic clicking, as if someone were tapping the metal box of the intercom post with a pin, a spike or even the sharp point of a fingernail which amplified and broadcast it to me. It was rhythmic and began to muddle my senses so I started to think it may just be some mechanical glitch interfering with the transmitter, that an electrical fault could be responsible for the gate bell's phantom ringing. There was no one there, I decided, even against the full rush of my better instincts.

I hung the receiver up, standing stock still for a few seconds. My breathing was a touch heavy, as if I had been holding air in my lungs all the while and it had seeped inwards, tensing my joints, my muscles.

'Who is it?' Dad called.

'It's no one again.'

'Just some damn *pecky* playing games,' he said, then added the phrase he often used in those situations, 'bloody *munts*.'

THAT NIGHT I didn't sleep much. The power remained out, the genny had been turned off so my stand fan didn't work. I stripped away my covers and lay on my bed bare-chested under a thin sheet but it was soon discarded, dumped like a rumpled rope beside me. Then I got up, opening all the windows as wide as I could. I even pulled the curtains away from the sides of the walls so the open space was fully exposed, a pointless attempt to allow more air in. There wasn't even the faintest midnight breeze. I lay on my side staring out at the darkness, the moonless black beyond the window frames, thinking about the expanses of infinity, and listening for sounds from outside. But there was silence. The only noises were those the house made, its routines, the rolling of water through the pipes, gravity filling cisterns, filling geysers, a creak in the rafters, the scatter of a rat. Or the dim slumbering moans through the walls that my miserable, hotly exasperated family were making. I tossed and turned in sympathy with them, then peeled off my silken briefs so I was lying naked. The freedom from all clothing was pleasurable, the sensation of being undressed against smooth Egyptian cotton forming a half-erotic image that skirted my mind, bringing some measure of imagined relief. I felt that first flush of arousal filter through me, my penis slowly distending, unhindered, away from my stomach, my hand already outstretched in automatic response, lowering itself towards my thin jutting shaft. I wondered whether I should chance my luck and message Amy, see if she was up, hot and bored too in her bedroom not thirty metres from mine. I could coax my late night mind to think on her, imagining her as I'd begun to that year. Or if I should flick on my phone and quickly bring myself off to one of those many steamy clips stored there, just a click away. Then my body began to heat through again, my skin grew clammy and I was beginning to sweat. The sheet beneath me dampened. Stuff it. I couldn't be bothered to do anything remotely heat-making, no matter how pleasurable. I thought over the day again, my shenanigans at the bottle store, my steamy arcs of piss sloshing down the President's face, those three men trailing up the hill behind me, eying me on their way down. I lay listening again in that now waning silence for the sounds that may drift to me from the street.

THE POWER CAME BACK just after midnight, thankfully whipping my fan into action, soon settling to a calming purr. I eventually slept on and off and the next morning, although it already seemed as hot as the night before, as if the earth and the air hadn't even cooled in the sun's brief hiatus, my mind at least felt clearer, cooler, less anxious. Sitting at the kitchen counter staring out the window at the crisp wash of caustic blue I could already anticipate the dread heat and fumy off-white haze of those impossible noon hours to come.

'This is ridiculous,' Becca said.

'Don't complain. You're the lucky one,' I said.

'How do you figure that?'

'You females don't have to wear a damn tie and thick socks all the way to your knees. Mom, this rule is so stupid. It's not fair. You should complain to the school.'

'Hey, don't call us "you females" as if we're some sort of lesser category of breeding livestock. Mom, tell him that's rude and sexist.'

I pulled a face at her. She raised her eyes at me. But I could see she wasn't in the mood for our usual early morning quick-fire exchange of sibling banter. She looked a little flushed and tired. She probably hadn't slept much either.

'Danny don't be rude about women,' Mom said, 'even if I tend to agree with you this time. You would think we lived in bloody Edwardian England the way we still carry on in this place.'

'See,' I said.

Becca didn't react.

Mom was bending down rearranging bowls and bottles in the fridge. 'Right I've got nice cold watermelon and cereal. I vote we skip the scrambled eggs and bacon today.'

We ate fat wedges of ice-crunchy melon, mine with a scattering of brown sugar. I followed it up with a milky bowl of cereal, but Becca ate nothing else. Petra waited to scoop away our plates as we finished eating and hobbled over with them to the scullery. She always had a habit of banging the plates just hard enough against the steel sink to drive Mom mad with annoyance. But that morning she let it go entirely, a first symptom of the energy-sapping day ahead.

33

'Remember Dad and I are going to the de Jong's for Diane's birthday dinner tonight,' she said, opening the freezer door. 'What do you two want Petra to make for supper?'

'Steak and chips,' I said.

'Okay, that works.'

She yanked a packet of frozen prime rump from an over-iced shelf. In the meantime Becca had shot a despairing look in my direction, her eyes widening.

'Aren't you going with?' she said.

'No,' I replied. 'I'm not going there, it's boring.'

But she was looking at me in a way which I felt was more a cue for help, a sort of silent pleading of the kind she'd been seeking from me far more often of late, drawing me in as a cool confidante in her life, a role I was rather liking. She had planned something in Mom and Dad's absence, it was clear, something having me around now threatened to derail. But the thought of a painfully drawn-out evening plonked in front of the de Jong's TV just killed me.

'I can't anyway,' I said, trying to suggest a compromise, 'I'm going to have loads of history homework. I'll be shut up in the study all evening trying to get it done. It'll take hours.'

'Fine,' Mom said.

I looked at Becca, a bit embarrassed, possibly for the first time in front of my big sister. She didn't look angry with me, but grimaced very slightly. She may have realised that I was trying to come up with a plan for her, assuring her I'd be well out of her hair for the evening. Or it may have escaped her altogether.

AMY AND BECCA went to the same girls' school, even though Becca was a senior in her last year and Amy was only a junior like me. Because we were old neighbours Becca gave Amy a lift every morning in her little pink Fiat. Sometimes as they chugged off I wondered what they said during the ten-minute trip. If they ever talked about me, whether Amy asked things about me only a sister would know? Maybe it was now awkward for Amy, being Becca's junior. Or perhaps they had no intention of speaking about me anyway.

She was always eager to ensure she never made Becca wait and was outside our gate by 6.55 on the dot. Mom urged her to ring on the intercom, come in for some tea or coffee, but I think Amy felt she shouldn't intrude first thing in the morning when other girls are maybe most blunt and bitchy. This suited me because I wasn't crazy at the thought of her entering my male space when I was busy deodorising myself or styling my hair in the bathroom mirror.

I would make sure I was ready early and when my nerve held firm I'd charge out the front door, dump my school bags by the Hilux and go out to see her. Our morning small talk was nothing very deep or serious. Usually there was a strange shyness about these greetings which eroded the flirty chattiness we shared if we had been messaging the evening before.

'Hey mister,' she said.

'Hi Amz. How are you?'

'I'm fine.'

'Another hot day.'

'Yeah, looks like it.'

'Yeah, yesterday was a bitch alright.'

'It was terrible,' she said. 'By the way Danny, someone's spray-painted your gate.'

AMY AND BECCA drove off, not very interested in the vandalism the black steel-plated surface of our gate had suffered. Dad and I stood looking at it. Dad was shaking his head, muttering to himself.

'Bloody fucking *munts*,' he said.

I knew he was mad because when he was really irritated he used the f-word in my presence. He never used it in front of my mom or sister, but with me I think he was trying to pass on some manly life-lessons, this time about it being okay to be pissed off when your private property's been defaced by lawless hooligans for no good reason. Signalling that I understood the code, I never baulked at hearing him use expletives, even when I was much younger, when such taboos registered as a shock. I kept stony, grim-faced, absorbing its seriousness and gravity.

'What does it say?' I asked, squinting. It wasn't very clear, scrawled with yellow spray paint used too sloppily, the edges and curves of each letter collapsed into a drippy mess.

'Looks like it says *hukuyu*,' Dad said.

'Not *huku*?'

'Dan, think my boy, why would someone right 'chickens' on our gate when I'm sure it's more meaningful and pointed to write 'beware,' hey?'

'I guess. But isn't *hukuyu* spelt *hokoyo*? And maybe 'chickens' could imply something as well. If you're chicken you're like lame at something, or scared.'

'No,' Dad said, 'it says *hukuyu*. I'm bloody sure it does.'

'But why?'

'Damned if I know. It's probably the start of the usual bloody election season intimidation, telling us whites to watch out, to stay out of it.'

'But why our gate I mean?'

'Probably just drunken thugs out late at night, picking a random target. The name Walker on our letterbox is a bit of a giveaway. Nothing to worry about. Just bloody pisses me off.'

'Yeah, typical.'

He turned and yelled for Ignatius. While our garden boy scurried towards us in his shorts and faded cream button-up cotton shirt to receive Dad's orders to wash and repaint the gate, I continued to look at the scrawl. I was tinged with dimming excitement, sensing the vandals had long moved on during the night without making any further commotion, that the vibrant strangeness of it was about to be covered in coats of blackness. It didn't occur to me at the time, later on in the day when I was catching a quick pee at the urinals between lessons, for instance, that this message could have been intended specifically for me.

SCHOOL WAS HOT AND DULL and by noon it was such a blanket scorcher that even our usually sour-faced maths teacher, Mr Maverick, told us to take off our ties, loosen our top buttons and use the lesson to 'quietly get on with other work'. In the last subject of the day, our Shona teacher, Miss Gwatidzo, didn't even try get us into the classroom. We headed straight down to the plush green lawns by the music department which were always shaded by an abundance of well branched leopard trees. We were meant to be 'practising Shona conversation, greetings and farewells' but no one could be bothered. She parked off on a concrete bench and fanned herself with an exercise book while we all splayed across the grass, mostly too hot to even horseplay around. There wasn't even a breeze to stir anyone to action. The air just incredibly still and clutching.

At lunch we saw the entire ranks of the swim team

splashing about in the pool and thought how lucky the bastards were. They were soon joined by several of the seniors who just stripped casually down to their briefs and jumped in, but we knew they'd never tolerate us juniors piggybacking on their crafty plan so we didn't even chance our luck. Standing outside the green palisade fencing looking in on the pool area, the wide expanses of shimmering water gave off that strong familiar chlorine tang with so many bodies thrashing around and this made me think of those long lazy Sundays splashing about the pool at home, for such long and indulgent periods my skin wrinkled over, my ears blocked and throbbing slightly.

'Why the hell did we idiots choose to do cricket?' my best friend Fruity said.

'Damned if I know,' I replied.

'Yeah, one lousy fucked-up decision.'

There was nothing to be done. We lugged our oversized cricket bags down the steps from the pool and slowly trailed them behind us towards the distant junior field, a place so out of the way its unimportance had earned it a nickname, the 'Cabbage Patch'. Along the way I dropped my bag and headed towards first sight of a tap. I had this sudden urgent brainwave to douse the base of my neck in a cold rush of water, the magic cure to my well-sunken fatigue, but when I clawed at the bronze handle it felt warm and I knew that whatever sloshed out the nozzle was going to be disappointingly tepid. There was something about the level of this heat which was so unusual that in my thirteen years I had never experienced anything like it or the feeling that its extremity was somehow displacing things, throwing the normal balance of our pretty ordered lives just a bit off kilter.

OUR STUPID MASTER-IN-CHARGE, Mr Carrick, made us practice catches in the shade of the line of fir trees which ran along the one far side of the Cabbage Patch. We did so lethargically and when one of us missed the ball and it breezed past an outstretched hand, we trailed after to retrieve it with about as much energy as a snail.

'Come on lads,' Mr Carrick said, 'try and put a bit of back bone into this session.'

'Yes sir,' we all muttered.

Yet no one was listening or intended to obey. Instead we stood about in a close semi-circle and one of us took it in turns to whack catches at the others at a force and speed so hard it bordered on being outright dangerous. It was aimed at making a point to Carrick, normally a stickler for getting on and doing things properly, by highlighting the farce of the whole thing, a game like cricket in deepest Africa, especially on this impossibly irritable day.

'Right, right,' he eventually said, 'if you lot can't concentrate and stop fooling about, just pack it in for the afternoon and bugger the hell off. See if I care.'

Cricket wasn't the natural choice of the black kids, yet we had a couple of them in our team. One was Taffy, a genuine star with a really great eye. We all adored him the way boys do, cussing the life out of him whenever we could. The other was a big deal of a guy from rich parents called James Sithole. He hung around us, or tried to, choosing to speak our style of lingo. He was what we called a 'coconut'.

We weren't that close so what he said to me as we were gathering up our cricket bags came as a surprise.

'Hey Walker, I'll be seeing you tomorrow night then.'

'What?' I said.

'Tomorrow evening you and your parents are coming

over to us for dinner. Don't you know? My dad and your dad are going to be business partners.'

The comment caught me off guard so I found myself looking at him, maybe squinting a bit, not really understanding.

'Don't look so surprised Walker. I mean it does happen that white men and black men work together these days. Don't you know?'

'Yeah, sorry, I just don't really know what you're talking about,' I said.

'Well don't sweat it, but I hear my dad's buying the majority stake in your dad's business. He told me last night. Apparently your dad's in a bit of trouble and needs my dad to bail him out.'

'Oh, really.'

'Yeah and I'm just saying I heard him talking about it, that's all. Nothing else.'

'Okay, well cool,' I said.

'Yeah, okay so check you later. I'll show you my pad and everything, it'll be awesome.'

He turned his right hand out as a gesture, his face focused for the moment, and I relented and high-fived him, but only after I held back for a second, this unsaid conversation still going on between us which hadn't quite finished, or hadn't really started at all.

'Later,' I said.

THE REST OF THAT LONG AFTERNOON I felt a touch ill, a bit queasy, but I don't think it was directly linked to the confounding idea of Dad and Mr Sithole being business partners, more the thought of it lingering in my head and the coincidence of something physical, probably a bout of genuine dehydration. I made sure I kept drinking large mouthfuls of bottled water. I mucked around with my friends for a bit while waiting to be picked up, but there was this syrupy lethargy covering everyone, and even the wide expanses of the playing fields spreading out around us gave off these sweltering waves which bathed us in an irritable stupor. On the way home I became further aware of this unsettled, dismal feeling which was more a low-grade brimming anger. I kept wondering whether Dad had really done some sort of a deal with James's father and what the awful degrading circumstances were. Some sort of uneasy negotiation might have taken place. Awkward exchanges, poker-faced glances, a distorted balance of power hovering between them. A long polished table in some corporate over air-conditioned boardroom, sitting across from one another, Mr Sithole in a tailored grey silk suit with a waistcoat even in the middle of summer, an elegant tie, expensive cufflinks. Dad in his usual chinos and a checked open collared cotton shirt. Sithole's chair one of those high-backed, wide-winged executive models, gold and gaudy trimmings. Dad's smaller, just ordinary, plain, basic. Or had it all been agreed upon on the side lines of one of our cricket matches, while James and I were toiling out on the field, easy and casual, a gentleman's handshake, a white hand gloved in a black one? It was all so quick, but had probably been a long time in the making and as usual Dad had kept it to himself. Mom would have known a bit, but not all the finer details. He'd disappointed me, let me down in some confusing way. I was ashamed of myself for thinking it, and sorry for him. I didn't say anything, it was an odd thought to digest, but I kept looking over at his featureless figure, obscured next to me in the late afternoon orange wash showering up from the dashboard and over him, wondering just what the hell he'd done.

I DIDN'T SAY ANYTHING, thinking instead this would warrant a big announcement at home, out on the veranda, Mom and Becca and me all summoned and assembled for a rare family conference, like the time we were told our grandma was ill and had only been given a few months to live. We were sure to be supportive, understanding of whatever reasons he chose to give us or didn't, no matter how surprising, illogical or unfair, knowing it was never our place to comment on such things or question him. Instead Dad and I drove through our freshly painted black gates and into the middle of an almighty punch up outside our front door.

'What the hell?' Dad said, seeing Mom and Becca, tightness shot through them both, waving their hands and yelling at Ignatius who stood some feet away, a slant in his posture, as if he were cowering, the hosepipe dangling from his hand. Petra was looking on from the steps by the front door, clutching a tea towel.

'I hope this isn't going to be some bloody domestic saga,' Dad said as we pulled up.

'Yes,' Mom said, moving towards us, 'now the boss is here so what are you going to say for yourself, hey?'

'Jenny, what's going on?'

'It's despicable,' Becca shouted before Mom could begin.

'What's happened?'

'He was spying on me, through my bedroom window, while I was changing.'

'What?' Dad said, turning towards Ignatius. 'What the hell do you think you're doing?'

'Nothing Boss,' he said, backing away, 'I was just watering like every afternoon.'

'He was staring in through my window! It was so obvious.'

'Hey, *mufana*, you just watch out. Okay? You hear me? I'll be watching you and you'll be out of here in a flash, like that,' he said, snapping his fingers, 'if there's even a suggestion you try that again. You hear me?'

Ignatius had steadied himself now, but for a big man he looked small and ridiculous, puzzled, mute. The hosepipe had channelled a steady flow into the rim of the flowerbed he had been watering and it looked like it was foaming, and it had drenched the legs of his blue overalls too as if he'd pissed himself. Maybe he had pissed himself by now.

'You hear me?' Dad yelled again.

'Yes boss,' he said, weakly.

'Now don't water round the front here when we're home, right, how many times do we have to bloody tell you? Go water round the back.'

'Yes boss.'

'Right go, move, you bloody *munt*.'

PETRA DASHED INSIDE, afraid she was next in the firing line, and disappeared out the back kitchen door. I traipsed in with my school bags and soon we were all reassembled in the hallway, the four of us, like a unit, a team, strength in numbers.

'Can you believe the cheek of it?' Becca said, a bit defensively now.

'He's got some nerve,' Mom added.

But Dad was furious.

'Don't be so bloody stupid,' he said, up close and direct to Becca. 'What the hell do you think you're doing getting changed with your bedroom window open? Just inviting bloody trouble that's all. Now wake up and don't be so damn naïve!'

'Yes dad,' Becca said, her head lowered in shame. 'I'm

sorry, it won't happen again.'

'Just think my girl.'

EVERYONE SLUNK OFF in different directions about the house. I was dying for a swim so I dumped my bags in my room, quickly stripped off, pulled on my swimming trunks and snatched the towel hung on the latch of my cupboard. I trotted outside towards the pool, relieved just to see that still clear water sunk there in our garden, some prized oasis in the funk of the dust-laden afternoon. I tucked my feet up to my chest and dive-bombed into the deep end, the water erupting over me as I felt my body slowing towards the bottom of the surface, cushioned in coolness. I resurfaced, my eyes filled with pool water which I flushed from my face with a thumb and forefinger. The dogs were yelping and darting round the edges like crazy, but I'd hoped my family would be fast on my heels, desperate to rinse the sweltering tempers of the day off their clammy skin. As I looked back towards the house I saw the glimmer of the pale slatestone surrounds of the pool, minute chintzes of minerals sharp and piercing in sun's pin-point intensity, then the flat run of browning lawn leading up to the abandoned veranda, the doors to the lounge open on some inner vacancy, with no sign or suggestion anyone was coming to join me.

TOWEL AROUND my waist, with damp feet, I tiptoed into the lounge, then down the passageway. Becca's door was closed and I presumed her to be sulking for a moment or nursing her embarrassment. She wasn't the sulky kind, but I didn't like it when something happened to fragment the family, an outburst, a snappy remark, a scolding, no matter how minor or short-lasting the rift would be. That bloody Ignatius, I thought, he was such a fool.

I wondered where Mom and Dad were. It was so hot indoors. Surely they were dying of thirst, craving their evening sundowners? I longed, urgently and desperately, for that crisp sound of a popping bottle top, the clinking of ice cubes in a glass, then the comforting silences following that first sip, signifying we were all content, nothing really needed to be said, discussed or set right. I crept further up the passage towards their bedroom. Their door was closed, itself an oddity, a bruising slap in the face, and behind it I could hear their muffled speaking. I couldn't make out their dull string of words, but I could hear that same levelled, graven tone from last night and immediately I knew what they were discussing.

Just fantastic.

I stormed outside. I thought about scaling the coffee shade tree to see if there were any signs of activity from next door, but I wasn't really in the mood now. I sat on one of the wicker chairs out on the veranda, towel still round my waist, my swimming briefs coolly and uncomfortably clinging to my thighs, and played with the dogs for a while.

'Danny you okay?'

It was Dad standing behind me, not that I'd heard him approach.

'Yes,' I said, 'I'm fine.'

'You sure?'

'Yes, Dad, I'm sure.'

THEY DID HAVE ONE DRINK OUTSIDE and even Becca came to join us. A usual family evening after all. It was all right now. Nothing more was said about the incident with Ignatius nor anything at all about the business deal and the bizarre prospect of going to James Sithole's place for supper the next night. It was another dry humid dusk, a frazzled blue dome above us dimming only slightly, bordered with a faint rim of rust coloured air, all that dust trapped under the heat. The odd tiresome comment about the punishing state of the weather mixed with mundane reports of the day was all that was really spoken about. Otherwise there was a pleasant kind of stillness, a restoration of sorts to the quiet state of calm I was more normally used to.

'Right you two, we'll be at the de Jongs' in case the power goes out and there isn't any phone signal,' Mom said in the hallway a bit later after Dad and she had dressed for going out.

'Okay,' Becca and I said.

'And if the power does go out, put the genny on Dan,' Dad added.

'Yeah,' I said.

'Don't stay up too late and make sure all your homework's done.'

'Yes mom.'

NO SOONER HAD THEY GONE, the gate bell rang. Oh God, not again, not this, I thought, starting out from my room but Becca strode past me in the passage. She pushed the button for the gate to open, not even asking who it was through the intercom, and the driveway soon flooded with that hard over-bright wash of headlights.

'Now Danny, you are going to be cool about this, right?' she said, turning to me. She looked and sounded like Mom. I was standing there staring back at her, not sure exactly what was happening.

'I mean you do understand, don't you? You're not going to be a little boy about this?'

I was taken aback by that suggestion.

'Of course not,' I said, 'do whatever you want, see if I care.'

She glared at me, hard for a moment, trying to cement my cooperation and also suggest in advance her disappointment if I let her down. Her eyes then softened, her face tilting, as if pleading.

'Don't worry,' I said, to assure her.

'Good. Thanks Danny. And you've got loads of history homework that's going to keep you glued to the study all night long, yeah?'

'Yeah,' I said, nodding my head sarcastically, 'loads and loads.'

WHEN I HEARD HIS VOICE from the driveway all sense of mystery evaporated. It was only Matt, my sister's boyfriend. I should have known and even felt stupid and childish that I hadn't expected he'd be over in a shot as soon as our parents went out. It was one of those tips I needed to store away, so that in future my sister needn't even mention it to me, I'd just act totally cool and unfazed, communicating my compliance by not communicating anything at all. As I stood there, feeling his presence grow larger up the walkway, Becca overcome with a battery of giggles, clutching onto him by the arm, I was stunned with this immediate panic. It was senseless because he'd been over to the house often, they'd been going out for at least three months already and still every time it happened, I was struck with this numbness in my mouth, a trembling from within. Matthew Chambers was a prefect at my school, a towering senior, a rugby first XV winger.

'Hey Dan the big man,' he said as he stepped inside, a beaming smile as he held his hand out to shake mine. He was tall and slim but well-defined, muscled. You could tell he was athletic. He had dark hair, gleaming green eyes, this tanned, completely smooth, unblemished skin. Becca and he made perfect sense, something of a golden couple, the ballet dancer and the rugby jock.

'Hi sir,' I said, feebly. His palm was strong but I tried hard to show him I had some strength in my grip too. Our eyes met briefly. I saw his gaze was searching me and I tried to avoid it. It was warm and stern at the same time, slightly disturbing. Then I realised that he was trying to tell me exactly what Becca had said before he came in.

'Hey, don't call me sir when we're not at school dude, it's completely cool.'

'Sure Matt,' I said, 'thanks.'

I BEAT A HASTY RETREAT to the study and even though I didn't have a scrap of history homework to do, I fiddled about on the computer, watching stupid clips on YouTube, sending a few messages on my phone, one to Amy, though she didn't reply, all the while a desk fan blasting fake air across me at full throttle, and I only resurfaced briefly when Petra called us for steak and chips.

LATER I GREW RESTLESS and padded down the passage virtually on tiptoes to find myself standing in Mom and Dad's room. Maybe boredom, maybe something else had drawn me there. The dual tall bronze bedside lamps spread a warm pale white light down on the black and orange bedspread with its tasteful ethnic swirls and squiggles, then up against the camel-cream walls before dimming outwards across the framed family pictures hanging on the wall, the refraction off the glass mostly obscuring our bright gleaming faces. I didn't need to see them to know they were there, the best lot of the several dozen of the four of us Mom was always snapping with some camera or another, convenient now with her iPhone, and then having them printed and framed for display there in the sanctuary of their bedroom, the real heart of our home, material evidence of our happy family quartet.

EVEN FROM THE STUDY, over the noise of the online clips and the beating of the fan, I was aware of the sounds of my sister and her boyfriend chatting, occasionally the odd howl or high-pitched screech of laughter carrying through to me, punctuating my disquiet. They had remained in her bedroom, but the door stood a touch open, intentionally I thought as I found myself coming out every so often to glimpse down the passage, as if to settle my inquisitiveness. It had worked, I didn't really mind. When we converged for dinner the chatter was subdued, jokey, gentle-natured and we all tried to make the best of an awkward situation, mostly snacking away in silence, Becca and Matt laughing and pinching one another or brushing their hands together every so often, before remembering I was present and making an effort to engage me. Mainly I tried to avoid looking at them. When Matt had come over for family dinners before it was easier because Mom and Dad acted as buffers, absorbing some of my unease. Now it was raw, a bit brutal. There had been music playing softly when they went back to her room, easy urban beats, more talk and laughter.

As I left Mom and Dad's bedroom, sure to straighten out their bedspread after I'd been lying on it for a short while, looking up idly at the white smoothness of the ceiling, I noticed that Becca's door was shut, the chatter had stopped and the music was off. Something told me they were still in there, they hadn't migrated to the lounge to curl up on the couch and watch TV or a DVD, and that the arrangement we'd seemed to have silently agreed on earlier had somehow shifted or been altered so that this new quietness was a disturbance to me, more testing than what they were doing before. I tiptoed past her bedroom door towards mine, at pains to be sure I couldn't be detected and accused later of some sort of creepy sabotage. I crept across my carpet and quietly curled up on my bed listening to that strange textured quiet. It was stuffy and putting my fan on would have made a noise so I soon slunk away, this time to the lounge where I skipped through channels, slouched in Dad's armchair, the volume down low.

THEIR QUIETNESS DIDN'T LAST LONG and I heard her door creak open and Matt's hurried voice saying he needed to be off, it was getting late, they had their 'fucking A levels to study for after all'. Becca laughed at this and he did too, but it was a short laugh now, stunted with truth. They didn't come to find me for him to say goodbye and I welcomed the escape from another uneasy exchange. I would see him at school the next day, where he'd no doubt be back to his fearful self, probably sure to stick me on manual if my shoes weren't polished mirror-like to specification or even take me behind the Common Room to give me a quick belt with a cricket stump to save the hassle of having to record it in the manual book. 'Fucking prick,' I hissed out aloud in the lounge, with some force, just above my breath. He and Becca were already out the door but I said it because I realised after all I was sore that he couldn't be bothered to look me in the face and say goodbye, maybe even an unsaid thank you for playing my part, for being a good sport. Instead he'd left and I felt certain I'd been used in some way, easily taken for granted.

BECCA CAME INSIDE and headed for the bathroom. I heard the taps open, drumming in the tub. When they finished running and I could hear her patting away in the water, I walked slowly into her room. The bedside lamp was on, the light dull and still. It seemed appropriate for an evening of romance. I noticed the odour of receded smoke, just a hint, mingled with a vanilla scent and saw a large squat candle standing on her dressing table. Even though the wick was extinguished and the wisps of smoke long trailed away, it gave off this sense of warmth, even if this was only imaginary, something seen in a movie. I rethought my perceptions about the light. It must have been more intimate, much darker, the candlelight flicker probably throwing some sort of incidental animation against her light cream walls, maybe across their skin. That's when I detected another smell in the room, one I was somehow familiar with. From where? It was vague but I was much younger, bursting into Mom and Dad's room on a Saturday morning, a stuffiness about the air, this clammy smell. It was the same here and I found myself looking down on Becca's bed, searching for patches of dampness, dampness I occasionally padded across on Mom and Dad's bed too on those weekend mornings. That old semi-familiar scent, a bit sour but not unpleasant, was the after smell of sex in a closed room, it must have been, and while realising this implication I noticed how hard I had become, very erect, this cringing exhilaration pumping through me.

A VISUALISATION PRESSED AT MY THOUGHTS though I tried to push it away. After Becca had finished bathing, I showered and then said goodnight to her. I half expected her to look different, or see her differently, in a new way, as if she glowed or there was a certain relaxation in her

51

posture, but there wasn't. She was back to her studies, arched over her books now at the dining room table, the stress of the senior student on her face, stitched in her brow, the worry of exams. I went to my room, put my fan on and lay about, thinking. It was pointless, my hard-on had come back, even as I turned from the dining room, walked down the passage I felt it rise and poke out at my cotton night briefs. I peeled them down now and hurriedly reached for my cock. Two or three hard strokes was all it took. I lay there after, my one hand groping my mouth, the joint feelings of shame and pleasure, then a more general disgust at myself, at everything I'd found out and been thinking about, followed by a sweaty heat all over me. Then I turned on my side and must have fallen asleep.

THE NEXT THING THAT HAPPENED was this almighty commotion the following morning. We had just finished breakfast and were getting ready for school while Petra was unlocking the front door as she always did first thing. There came these sharp, wild, punctuated screams ranging out all over the house, the likes of which we'd never heard before, probably not even on horror films. Dad came storming down the passage, shirtless, while Mom stood in the kitchen, paralysed to respond. I followed Dad out into the hallway.

'What the bleeding hell?' he said.

Petra was on the lawn beside the walkway to the front door, her hands clutched to her mouth, shrieking, her cries so high pitched they were genuinely ear-piercing, followed by these almost breathless gasps, her chest heaving in and out. Her movements were something like a gyration, frantic and crazed, but when I could see her face long enough I realised she was truly stricken with deep panic.

Dad saw this too. 'Now just calm down,' he said, moving towards her, trying to grab hold of an arm so he could steady her. 'It's alright old *ambuya*, you're okay. Nothing's going to harm you.'

But as he approached she turned and fled, making a beeline round the back of the house, her spindly legs making quite a go, yells and screams trailing behind her.

'Jesus Christ,' Dad said, turning to me, looking as mystified as I was. 'What the hell has gotten into the bloody old *munt*?'

I shrugged my shoulders.

'Love,' he shouted, but Mom and Becca were already standing in the doorway, their faces etched with slightly detached fright.

'What's gotten into her?' Mom asked.

'Something's obviously upset her like crazy. Better try to see if we can calm her down. She might even be having some sort of seizure, or a fit of some kind.'

'God almighty,' Mom said, turning back towards the kitchen.

Dad and I went after her, out the back into the courtyard, then down towards the *kias*, but she'd moved away into the bottom of the garden where Mom had caught up with her and managed to hold onto her by the shoulders. She had collapsed to her knees and Mom held her head steady against her thighs and was stroking her head, the side of her face, trying to pacify her. Tears were streaming down her cheeks as she rocked back and forth, stiff and robotic, her eyes wide and glaring at some unseeable horror. She was chanting something in Shona, spitting out the words, a deep rasping from the back of her throat, the same phrase over and over.

'COME AND LOOK AT THIS,' Becca called to us.

Dad and I strode back round to the front of the house. The dogs were trotting around, ready to play. Becca was pointing to something by the front door, placed there in a row on the edge of the single wide step, inconspicuous to us.

'What is it?' I asked.

They were balls of long bush grass, four of them, roughly palm-sized, definitely shaped and woven by hand. Through the centre of each one, inserted into the apex of these grassy globes, were two narrow sticks, tied at their centre with layers of black thread, making the shape of an X.

'*Juju*,' Dad said.

IGNATIUS SWORE BLIND it wasn't him. Dad summoned him thinking it was some sort of retaliation for the incident over Becca's bedroom window, a way of threatening us. But by now Ignatius had heard the commotion and was hiding in the shower cubicle of the *kia* refusing to come out, muttering something similar to what Petra was.

'Not me,' he said in between this, calling through the door, 'I am not the one, no, no.'

Dad had had enough now.

'Fine,' he said, throwing his arms up, 'I've had it up to here with you bloody *munts*. All you do is cause bloody dramas all damn day long. I think it's high time we sacked the bloody lot of you and got on with things our self!'

He stormed back into the house, coming out again with a gas lighter and the four grass balls clutched to his chest.

'Daniel come here,' he said, 'hold these will you.'

We stood by the old upturned petrol drum we kept at the back of the garages where we occasionally burnt old rubbish. One by one Dad tore apart the grass balls, ripping out the X signs, snapping the twigs. Then he flicked on the gas lighter and set all the grass ablaze, dropping each bundle into the drum. It was so dry it all caught alight instantly, in mere seconds completely incinerated.

'And that's what I think of their fucking *juju* and their fucking African customs and all that crap,' he said to me as we walked back to the house, wiping his hands together to flick off specs of ash.

THE LAST I SAW OF THE SAGA, Petra had been coaxed to sit on the step outside the backdoor of the kitchen and Mom had draped a blanket over her. She was shaking and muttering and Mom was trying to soothe her, rubbing her shoulders. Dad was annoyed with her for showing this degree of sympathy because he didn't say much to her as we left the house for school, forgoing his usual quick kiss on the lips and squeeze of the arm to wish her a good day.

SCHOOL WAS DULL AFTER THAT. Then it became hot and dull. Very hot. I spent all day trying to dodge Matthew Chambers which I succeeded in doing, maybe because he was trying to dodge me too, but I didn't manage to avoid James Sithole who shared a number of my classes and kept making chirps about how I was coming over to his place for supper, how he was going to show me his 'pad'.

'What the hell's he on about?' Fruity asked me after the fourth time James made a comment. He was a little taken aback even by the thought of me going there.

'Don't even fucking ask,' I said.

I FINISHED MID-AFTERNOON, after my French tutorial, and Becca came to pick me up. In the car I didn't say much to her, not sure if she knew what I knew, but my silent indifference was in some way quite powerfully telling, showing her I didn't like being taken advantage of, coaxed into secret, and I could be a threat to her, in some way or another. Even if that's not exactly what I felt, I was certain I had gained the upper hand between us. She appeared to be in such a good mood, playing Adele songs loud from her phone through the iTrip, singing, 'There's a fire, starting in my heart / Reaching a fever pitch, it's bringing me out the dark' and as she did she looked across at me, smiling playfully and willing me, moving her head from side to side, her left hand pinching my thigh, and so I relented and joined in with, 'We could've had it all, rolling in the deep ...' We packed out laughing and she turned the volume up even louder as we sped home. I wondered if that's what proper sex does to you, makes you happy, puts you in a good mood? It must do, I thought, or else why would everyone be doing it all the time, why was it such an obsession? Then I realised I was wrong and she was right. I was still just the small kid, the younger brother, and I would do anything for her, anything at all, and perhaps now she knew that I knew this.

AT HOME PEACE SEEMED to have been restored. Petra was skulking in the scullery, scrubbing the big aluminium pot she used to broil the dogs' bones in while Ignatius was around the back clipping the bougainvilleas. I could hear the snip-snip of the large shears from the kitchen where I poured myself a tall glass of pear juice, shoving in a handful of ice cubes. I had some homework to do which I wanted finished as soon as possible so I settled at my desk, my school shirt discarded, the fan angled towards me, breezing pleasantly enough on my bare skin. Becca did a quick change into her ballet attire and shouted bye to me on her way out again. When I finished my work I shoved on my swimming trunks and chucked myself into the pool, thrashing around a bit, teasing the dogs, until I heard the gates roll open and saw Mom's white Honda CRV glide up the drive. It must've been after four.

WE HAD TEA AND BISCUITS out on the veranda but Mom didn't say very much, not even about going to the Sithole's for supper when I told her what James was on about. 'Oh yes,' she said, 'didn't I tell you? Just a business obligation of your father's. They've specifically invited you so it would be rude not to go. Plus James is a friend of yours, isn't he?' The way she fobbed it off annoyed me so I didn't respond, but blew air into my cheeks and tried not to shake my head so she'd notice. She said we were leaving at six-thirty and to be sure I was ready on time. Then I slid away to my room. I intended to sulk for a bit, make something of a protest that I was just expected to go along and have bloody James Sithole show off in my face the whole damn night. I doubt Mom would have sympathised. The way she announced it, lacking any trace of enthusiasm, gave away her own apprehensions and I realised we were comrades in arms as far as this all went.

Instead I was distracted by the arrival of a message. It was from Amy saying she was sorry she didn't reply to me last night but she'd heard me in the pool and wondered whether I wanted to meet her over the wall in our usual place. Cool, I replied, see you there.

I didn't bother to change from my damp swimming trunks but sprayed some deodorant under my arms and across my torso before scooting out. I hopped onto the coffee shade tree, leapt on top of the durawall and flung myself over, landing on the hard sun-baked webbed red soil which stung the soles of my feet. Amy was already waiting for me, wearing tight fitting blue shorts and a pale yellow spaghetti top. We giggled as a greeting, marvelling at our secret rendezvous. These meetings of ours, as occasional as they were, were watershed moments, highlights amidst weeks of tedious home routine, school, sport. We huddled down behind the heap of the rockery, quickly beginning to joke and gossip. I told her all about the drama with Petra and the freaky balls of grass, which she said her family had heard from their yard.

'No ways,' she said, putting her head back in laughter, 'that's brilliant. I can just imagine her dancing around the garden like something possessed by voodoo.'

'Yeah, it was hysterical,' I said, 'you should have seen the look on her face. It was completely demented.'

'Brilliant,' she repeated, rubbing her hands together.

We chatted more, leaning against the wall, enjoying the mild coolness of the coffee shade tree which towered and sprawled its network of branches and thick leaves above us.

Without warning she leaned over and placed a hand on my abdomen, flat on my bare skin. It was warm. Her skin, her palm and fingers, were incredibly smooth.

'You have such a nice tan, Danny,' she said, beginning to move the flat of her hand over my stomach, then my chest, brushing over my pecs which I was trying to flex without making it apparent, while attempting, too, to hide my lean-boned skinniness.

'Thanks,' I said.

Then she brought her face closer to mine to initiate a kiss and slowly we began to make out, an even rarer delight for us during these encounters. It was an awkward coming together of lips, in this unspoken moment of agreement, unfolding unpredictably, very tensely, every time initiated by her, a boldness I lacked. There was nothing official between us, no agreement that we were in any way a couple or an item. We were just a boy and a girl, and what was happening was in defiance of our long history as childhood friends, our endless playing together, child's stuff, getting dirty, roughed up, riding our bikes like *skelems* about the neighbourhood, swimming or mucking around in either one of our gardens, playing cruel pranks on the servants and their *piccanins*. Now she didn't do any of that and I had started to see her in a different light, as she probably saw me, judging by the way she kept lightly caressing my stomach and chest, a bit ticklish though I was trying to be serious about it, not break down in a fit of giggles.

All this was only natural, I thought, let it happen.

I slid my right hand up her back on the outside of her spaghetti top and gently rested there against her, feeling the pressure of her body move against it, easing into the shape of my rigid palm. Nothing seemed to guide me. All the gigabytes of porn I had digested, all I thought I knew about sex didn't even register as the same thing, there in the actual long-held moment of being intimate with a girl. I was only thirteen and all of that business shouldn't have been pressing on me anyway, its happening was for another time, the wonder years to come, no matter how much I'd already fantasised and imagined it, suffered the urges.

I lost my nerve and broke away from the sweet taste of her moist lips, which I'm sure she had glossed with something like apple cherry, sitting back against the wall.

'Hey Amz,' I said, recalling what I'd been meaning to ask her when we next met, 'I don't suppose you want to come with me to our end of year junior dance next Friday, do you?'

'Of course, I'd love to,' she said, playfully slapping my thigh, 'what the hell has taken you so long to ask, mister, I've been waiting for ages.'

'Oh, I'm sorry.'

'A girl needs time to prepare, don't you know?'

'Yeah,' I said. 'That's so cool. We'll have a blast.'

I leaned over to give her one more short kiss on her cheek before jumping up, scaling back over the wall and scarpering away to the house, knowing already, a bit disheartened to think it, that several days would probably pass before our next communication, and that we'd most likely avoid any reference to what had happened, seeing it as a violation of the rules of friendship, a once-off that wasn't supposed to happen, except of course we both knew that it was.

I TOLD MOM, a bit nervously when I was back at the house, and she threw her hands up, this wide and wild animated look instantly taking over her face. She flung her arms around me, pecking me repeatedly on the cheeks.

'Mom!' I said, wiping my face, 'cool it will you. It's no big deal.'

'Danny, Danny, Danny, your first real date. What a charmer you are!'

'Jeez Mom, relax,' I said, moving away towards the passage.

'We'll have to match up your outfits. I'll get hold of Monica right away and we'll plan it all out. What fun!'

'God I never should have told you,' I called to her.

LATER A STRANGE old *madala* was sitting on a small wooden stool by the *kia*, leaning his back against the whitewashed wall. I noticed him when I went into the courtyard to fetch my swimming towel from the washing line. It was odd because Dad didn't allow anyone else onto the property, and the staff had to go out onto the road to see their *shamwaris*.

This *madala* was very old with completely white hair and a white beard, rare for African men. He wore a white full-length robe, tied round the waist with a rope, the ends dangling beside him with tassels, sandals on his feet. Propped against the wall was a long stick with a fat knob on the end. He looked right out of a documentary re-enactment of the life of Moses. He was resting his head back against the wall, his body slack, dozing.

'Who's the old *madala* by the *kia*?' I asked Mom out on the veranda.

'Apparently the apostolic prophet,' Mom said. 'Don't ask. Petra's insisting on him. He's here to cleanse the house after this morning's incident.'

'Bloody cheek if you ask me,' Dad said.

'Don't cause a fuss,' Mom said. 'Just let it happen.'

Dad shook his head, clenching his jaw.

'It's just a blessing, a few words anyway. You know how they are with their beliefs. Besides she's never going to put a foot out of the kitchen again if we don't do something.'

'So she's calling the shots now is she?'

'She's petrified, the poor old girl. She's already refused to go anywhere near the hallway all day and I'm not about to don a *doek* and apron and start doing the cleaning and sweeping myself thank you very much.'

'Never know, might suit you, love,' Dad said, winking at me.

'Yeah, Mom, it might be the new "it" look,' I added.

'Hey, you two, just watch it will you.'

We chuckled at the thought.

WE HAD TO WAIT for Becca to come back from her dance class at five-thirty because the cleansing ritual didn't work unless we were all there. We assembled outside the front door, the four of us, a timid looking Petra and Ignatius, even the dogs sat about. The old *madala* stood very straight and tall, an air of authority about him you couldn't deny, this wise old man. His eyes were black marbles, his gaze gripping and powerful. Even Dad was on guard, watching what he said, exercising patience. For us it was more of a spectacle, a bit of a joke of the 'only in Africa' category that would make a great tale to tell friends over a *braai*, but I could see why it might be different for the blacks. When he stamped his stick on the brickwork, Petra immediately fell to her knees and then Ignatius kneeled, though I could tell he wasn't as sold on the whole palaver.

The old *madala* started speaking, serene words, reassuring in their tone. He was talking in Shona and drew signs in the air with his stick, clutched in a very stiff, straight arm. He outlined an imaginary circle round the area on the step where the balls of grass had been. His words intensified, becoming faster, louder, his gaze set on the four of us more closely. Petra began shaking her head, eyes closed, muttering something under her breath while the rest of us stood round silently, looking on.

A slight change of tone came about, and I couldn't bring myself to look him in the eye any longer. He wasn't speaking in Shona now, but veered into some other language I'd never heard before, something mystical, even in tongues. Dad was becoming impatient but it didn't last much longer, concluding with a tap for each of us on the forehead very faintly with the knob of his stick. Oh shit, not good. I thought Dad would clobber him. He didn't, he stood there, letting it happen. The old *madala* bowed his head to us and fell silent.

'Thank you,' Mom whispered. It had become odd, even embarrassing to be standing there for some ritual none of us believed in for a second.

We all dispersed but the old *madala* hung around, looking as if things weren't quite finished. Petra whispered
something to Mom.

'Oh,' she said, 'right, okay.'

She went into the kitchen and came back out with half
a loaf of bread, a tin of sweetcorn, two cans of Coke and a
bottle of beer. The old *madala* clapped his hands in thanks,
a broad smile coming across his face, and took off towards
the gate.

Dad was standing there. Christ, bloody typical, I thought
he would say. He didn't say anything.

I WENT FOR A SHOWER, then lay on my bed. I had barely
dried, just patted myself with a towel, wanting to retain
that snappy coolness your skin feels when coming out of hot
water. Even though I'd just soaped and scrubbed myself, I
felt myself sweating, my skin clammy already. I turned the
dial on my fan to max. The thought of torturing my body
by snuffling it in trousers and socks and shoes was killing,
the effort unfathomable. I lay there for a bit longer, my
thoughts returning to Becca, how she'd be home alone the
whole night. She said she had no plans to do anything but
study. Yeah, right. Sure she did. I bet the gate bell would
ring the moment we were gone and Matt would zoom up
the drive, eager and ready. I thought of her room again,
that head-filling smell I was so sure was the hanging odour
of just finished sex, what is cast in the air when bodies come
together, the friction of skin on skin, when fluids leak. It
worried me and then it didn't, just as I toyed with the idea
of alerting my parents to her secret, pulled to that childlike
habit of obligation and rightness, then thought, *don't you
dare, you little fag.*

WE WERE OUT THE GATE at six-thirty, hot in the Hilux, even with the air con up high, on our way to the Sitholes. We straightened out onto the dual carriageway of Borrowdale road, soon settling into cruise mode, weaving in and out of traffic.

'Dan,' Dad begun, 'just so you know, an opportunity came up to do a bit of business with Julius Sithole, okay, that's why we're going round there tonight.'

'Okay,' I said.

'It's just customary, a show of good faith, help establish a good relationship and all that.'

'It's called etiquette, Danny,' Mom said.

'Yeah, okay.'

But Dad continued. 'It's just business, strategic if you like, nothing more.'

'Okay,' I said again.

'Things are a bit unsettled in the country right now, you know, if you want to survive out there you need to make friends with the right people. Well, just so you understand, Dan. Just so you don't pick up the wrong idea.'

'It's cool dad.'

'You sure?'

'Sure,' I said.

He drove on, but he was eyeing me out occasionally in the rear-view mirror, looking back at me, glowering slightly, narrowing his eyes, as if to say, now don't go being a moody little shit all night mister! I hadn't wanted to talk about it then. It was all a bit late in the day, I thought, the deal must've been on the table for weeks, why hadn't he bothered to talk to us about it before now? But what did it really matter? This was how things worked in our country, nothing was ever straight forward, not remotely, and Dad knew that better than anyone.

I sat back, breathed out. It was beginning to dim, the light over the suburbs going hollow and behind us a huge red blazing disc was busy plummeting into the far distance, somewhere over the unmanned savannah. When I turned briefly to look out the window I still had to shade my eyes from the sun's intensity even though there were ripples and waves of crimson filtering outwards, softening the edges of that hard rainless summer light.

THEN A FEW MINUTES LATER Mom said, as if she'd been keeping it in for a long time and now needed to get it off her chest, 'I just hope you're doing the right thing Dave.'

'Done the right thing,' Dad said, after a pause, patting Mom's knee to assure her. 'The deal's been done, remember, tonight is just all for show, to show me who's boss now, the big man up in his palace.'

I could hear Mom sigh. She lowered her head a bit. There were traces of faint tears forming in the corners of her eyes. I was suddenly attentive now, sitting forward slightly, leaning in towards the two of them, into the path of this brimming disquiet.

'Anyway it's all symbolic, political, you know why. Plus he won't be around to show much of an interest. We're far too small for him to really be worried about. Just think of it as banking a nice cheque and getting a highly connected black business partner while the going's good … and willing.'

'He owns the bank that the cheque came from!' Mom said, sarcastically, 'and you didn't leave it in there for very long, did you?'

'Different reasons, Jenny.'

'My foot. You cashed the entire lot the second the deal was signed. The ink hadn't even dried. What does that say about the amount of trust you have in your new business partner?'

Dad shrugged. 'No banks are safe right now. It's an election season. Who knows what these goons might say or do? So any capital is better off in cash. And you're damn right, I have about as much trust in Julius Sithole as I do in the average bloody *munt* on the side of the road, no further than the end of my bloody nose.'

That put an end to it until we reached a major intersection and came to a stop at a traffic light. As we were waiting we noticed this huge new billboard towering over the entire width of the intersection, erected on scaffolding. It was lit up from below with beaming angled spotlights, the brightest thing around by far in the late falling dusk. There was a picture of the President to the one side, his fist clenched, and next to it in large black ink it said, 'INDIGENISATION = POWER TO THE PEOPLE', while underneath was sprawled, '*Say No to Western Imperial Forces! Resources Belong to the People! Vote for Sovereignty, Vote for Emancipation!*' To the side rested the old party logo in yellow, green and black.

I could see Mom and Dad take it in for a moment, absorbing its brashness. They were sitting there side by side, this quiet fury riling through each of them, a quick hard glance to one another, exiting a moment later at Dad's face with a short chuckle and dismissive shake of the head. Their earlier conversation had restarted, the billboard proving a point, and this was Dad's way of conceding, in part, that what he'd done was indeed a risk. But also that everything was a risk, so there was a chance he was right too. I was studying that blown-up photograph closely, those square glasses, the two stark eyes behind them, the pursed lips, the little snip of a moustache. A flashback zoned across me, the sensation of standing there blissfully pissing over that muscular face, provoking an anger, or if not directly there and then, the feeling I was contributing to a bigger anger somewhere, a more general widespread resentment. We seemed to hover there forever, poised at that red light, that busy intersection, but finally we crossed and were on our way up into the new suburbs where the mansions of the Fat Cat Cronies, as Dad called them, were scattered across the green hilltops.

WE STRUGGLED TO FIND THE ROAD for the Sithole house. It seemed intentionally difficult to work out, not signposted, off an obscure side lane, very badly potholed, which didn't appear to be a proper road at all. Eventually, at the end of a long winding drive up and down what was an ever expanding *kopje*, past property after property with expansive high walls and fancy entrances, some of which were just stark building sites, we came across their number and turned into their driveway. It had a massive gridded gate, not a solid one like ours, at least three metres high, arched at the top. There were these big concrete statues of lions with their mouths wide open, as if roaring, at the base of two enormous pillars stretching up either side of the entrance. It was all painted in very subtle pink, including the wall stretching out on either side of the gates, the pillars, the lions, even the paving stones glinted in a kind of milkshake pink.

'Oh my God,' said Mom.

She wasn't talking about the gate, the lions, the pinkness of everything, but what lay beyond. We sat there for a moment, allowing the Hilux to idle so we could take it all in. It was like a showy corporate exhibition, but staged just for the three of us, and whoever else might just happen to drive by this quiet, remote suburban street. Directly ahead at the end of the run of short paving there was a wide parking bay, beyond it a long row of garages or a showroom displaying five gleaming, very expensive vehicles, models the like of which you didn't normally see about our town, each the most brilliant diamond white. They faced us, their sleek black wheels slightly angled for added effect. They weren't locked away out of sight, but displayed behind clear Perspex or some sort of heavy duty glass. Each cubicle was lit up with piercingly sharp spotlights, shining this shower of bright white light, rebounding off the crisp white painted walls of the garage interior. Framing each of the five slabs of Perspex was a rim of fluorescent lighting which pulsed the weakest neon blue.

'Well that's one way of showing your rich neighbours how much richer you are than them,' Dad muttered, leaning out the window to press the intercom. The gates divided in the middle, drifting soundlessly apart. 'Right, remember this guy is a heavyweight in the party, so let's all watch what we say, alright?'

'Alright,' Mom and I said.

THE HOUSE DIDN'T APPEAR that big from the front, just a long, elegant single storey building, painted in the same light pink which up close may have been a tinted off-white, but it had massive double teak front doors with brass etchings nailed onto them, brass lion heads as door knockers. Maybe lions were the Sithole totem? There was no one there to meet us so we stood out on a smooth white concrete slab until Dad gently knocked. A maid opened at once, curtseying, gesturing we follow her through this huge hallway. Everything was decorated in shades of white, ivories, creams, silvers. It all shone, giving the impression there was glass everywhere, or even mirrors, so you weren't sure what you were seeing was real or a reflection of something else. The floor was tiled with large glassy squares that had a slightly speckled sheen, and even those seemed to reflect back your murky deformed shadow as you walked along. We entered into a massive room with high ceilings, very plush furniture, glass chandeliers and lamps, with several Zebra skins on the floors. All five of the Sitholes were arranged round a long L-shaped sofa, the men standing, the ladies sitting, beaming at us as if they were posing for a photoshoot spread in a glossy celebrity magazine. After very warm greetings and introductions, they led us out to a wide terrace where there was a bar by an infinity pool which plunged into another wider pool beneath it, more terraces, then something further beyond that, the dark muscled gleam of a reservoir or a small dam. That's when we saw the full extent of the mansion, tumbling and sprawling another three or four layers down the side of the hill, a huge clutter of buildings. Beyond all this was a panorama of clustered city lights. There was the feeling you were elevated, above everything.

MR AND MRS SITHOLE were very nice people. I had seen them before at school. Mr Sithole was a bit chubby, bald, always grinning. Mrs Sithole was tall, elegant with long hair extensions, impeccably dressed in something very chic looking. Apart from James there was his older brother Jasper who was back from his university studies in Cuba and their sister Julia who was sixteen and went to Becca's school. Her mom made her play the flute for us before dinner, which she did reluctantly, claiming she was useless, until she played, sounding faultless.

'Jules has just passed her grade six exam in flute and grade seven exam in piano,' Mrs Sithole said, as we applauded, 'both with distinctions!' She gestured over to the corner of the room where a polished black baby grand piano stood. 'I make her practise for at least an hour a day. She plays wonderful Bach and Schubert, Mrs Jepson, her teacher, tells me, and can play five octaves of scales with both hands in every key.'

'Mama, please!' Julia whispered, 'don't embarrass me.'

'You're very talented,' Mom said.

I PAIRED OFF WITH JAMES early on in the evening, leaving the grown-ups to their talk. 'We can hang out in my room, it'll be dope.' As we descended flights of stairs into this warren of wide passage ways, through the differing splendour of various reception rooms, I began to dread the idea of being in his domain, having to concede that it was so much bigger and better than mine. I thought this was all he was after, trying to lure me there, deeper into the mansion's vast interior, so far inside its maze of rooms I wouldn't find my way back to the adults. Then he could extract that confession from me, even just by sensing it in my reaction, an admission that what he had *was* bigger and better than what I had.

It turned out to be a fairly modest-sized room, though he did have his own en suite bathroom which I had to admit was really cool.

'I have to share with my annoying sister,' I said. 'And trust me, women take hours in the bathroom!'

'Yeah I guess it's nice to have,' he said, but not in a boastful way. He was more interested in showing me his collection of butterflies which were contained in three enormous frames hung in a straight line on a wall over a lengthy pine desk.

'Check this out,' and he flipped a switch, revealing very effective backlighting simultaneously lighting up all three frames, exposing a multitude of patterns and colours on the velvety specimens pinned up in very ordered rows.

'Neat,' I said.

'It was my main hobby when I was a lightie. I managed to collect a specimen of every species known in the country, male and female, except for one, the *Mylothris rueppellii haemus* from the Pieridae family. That's 526 different species of butterfly.'

'No way.'

'And the *rueppellii* is actually quite a common butterfly, but for some reason it eluded me. I think I was growing out of it as a hobby by then, to be really honest and I kind of lost interest.'

'Oh, right.'

'Yes, it's not a terribly exciting pastime if you think about it.'

'I guess.'

Despite this odd fastidious display, his room wasn't out of the ordinary. It was neatly kept, but not too neat and that made me feel a little easier, pleased at the thought that maybe there wasn't this host of servants frantically picking up after him 24/7. There were posters he'd hung on the walls of rap stars, super cars, cricket players. One was a framed autographed poster of Chris Gayle. Scrawled in black ink, it said, 'What up James, keep it real ya, Chris Gayle.' He had a hat stand with a collection of expensive brand label hats and caps, including a Baileys, a Barbour and a pale blue New Era, which I impulsively tried on in a tall mirror that hung beside them. He didn't seem to mind.

He did have a TV and a gaming consul, so we lazed on these funky bright green and blue bean bags playing games for a bit, but he bored pretty quickly, so he switched it off and instead Bluetooth'd some urban R&B beats from his phone to a set of amazing Klipsch speakers discreetly installed about the room.

'You've got a dope crib,' I said.

'Thanks, it's decent.'

We let the music swell the atmosphere a bit, casually nodding our heads to the beat.

'Hey Danny.'

'Yes.'

'I'm pretty grateful you came.'

'It's no sweat James.'

'Normally when daddy has one of these business dinners I get sent down here to do boring studying.'

'Oh right, that's shit.'

'Yes, but this evening, because it's your dad my dad is bailing out, mama said I could have the night off from work and hang out with you.'

'Yeah, it's cool.' Then I said, 'but what do you mean your dad is bailing out my dad?'

'Nothing. Well it's just what he does. He owns a bank, don't you know?'

'Yeah, and?'

'Well he helps businesses in trouble, bails them out, puts up capital.'

'But he's becoming a partner, so it's not in trouble, he's getting something back.'

'Well he only does it because he's connected and your dad's, well he's a whitie, he needed a black partner or else.'

'Or else what?

'His company would've been taken over anyway, by the government.'

I looked hard at him for a moment, biting back against an instant swell of resentment which had probably been building between us for some time. Then I said it. 'James, my dad says your dad's bank is crap and he wouldn't trust him for a second, so don't go thinking he's out and about saving the bloody country by splashing some money around.'

'Hey, that's not what I meant Walker, take it easy dude.'

'Yeah, well he's already withdrawn all that money your dad gave him for the deal because he says that bank's dodgy and about to go bust.'

James looked at me, his eyes burning, but it wasn't with the raw defensive anger I expected, more a spooling look of despondency, disappointment, as if his plans, which had started well enough, suddenly weren't going right for him. Then he fiddled on his phone, changing the music.

'You like Drake?' he said.

'Yeah,' I said, shrugging my shoulders, 'I guess.'

LATER, BACK OUT ON THE LARGE top terrace, where the adults were having cocktails and Dad and Julius were puffing a fat cigar together, chuckling over golf stories, I did something very mean to James Sithole, very unnecessary. An uneasiness had slipped between us after that conversation in his room, not unexpectedly, so all through dinner the remnants of it kept surfacing in the quiet resolve which settled over us youngsters. Sometimes Jasper spoke about Cuba and how he was training to be a doctor there, and Julia seemed sometimes interested and sometimes not, but James and I sat across the table playing this staring one another out game, a challenge which had no point to it, but a stupid way of raising our eyebrows and smirking when either of our fathers said anything which suggested one had outdone the other, as if we were scoring points. It was childish and pathetic, an imitation really of how childish and pathetic our fathers were being too. I knew it even at the time, cringing as I kept on goading him, going a step further, but that's not the mean thing I did, just a prelude to it.

73

Outside after dinner he was sitting on a sunlounger, quite far apart from the others, not within earshot of anyone. I sat next to him, pulled out my phone, punched in the pin number, flicked through messages. I made out that I was writing someone a text, but I made sure he could see that I was open at the secret WhatsApp group, an image of one of those explicit pics plainly visible.

'Hey, what's that?' he asked.

'Nothing. Just a group us guys at school belong to,' I said, moving closer to him, making sure he could clearly see. 'It's pretty cool. Here have a look if you want.'

He took my phone and started scrolling through the collection.

'Don't worry,' I said, 'the volume's off.'

He tapped the 'play' arrow on a video and I watched him watch it, his eyes narrowing in, holding the screen a bit closer to him. His face gradually lit up with that look of hot, horny, forbidden excitement.

'Can I join the group?' he asked.

I paused before responding, as if seriously considering it, even giving him a sense of false hope. 'Hey, I'm not sure. I can ask the others, but they're pretty strict rules about who belongs. And, you know, it's kind of exclusive.'

I watched him to see what his reaction was, whether I'd landed a hard cruel blow, made him realise that despite all he had, his big house and daddy's wealth, he just wasn't one of us.

He didn't react at all. It was possible he knew what I was up to and had thought of a way to outsmart me. 'Man I just love white pussy,' he whispered, slowly, shaking his head. 'Yes, man. White pussy is the deal. Imagine beating off to this hottie.'

MOM INSISTED SHE DRIVE HOME because Dad had had several of the expensive single malt Scotch on the Rocks Julius insisted they knock back to toast the deal. No one said much at all on the drive down. By all accounts the Sitholes had been very gracious, attentive hosts. The food was amazing and I'd eaten so much I was heavy and tired, dozing in the back. The drive seemed long, the roads dark and desolate now, but then some time later a shudder of an image rolled past the window and in an instant I was alert, turning my neck to follow it, trying at the same time to regain my bearings. We were very near home, in fact on Alice Smith Road, clawing up the hill. I was sure we'd just passed those three men in blue overalls, the same men who seemed to follow me back from the bottle store. I was certain it was their swagger, the distinct make up of that trio, blurring past us, perhaps a can of paint between them, intent to go about their mischief, that potent legend *hokoyo* again sprayed and suspended on the hot black surface of the night. Be careful. Be warned. But when I tried to shuffle round on the seat to see for sure, there was just a stretch of darkness behind us.

FULLY AWAKE, a different thought occurred to me as we were about to turn into our driveway.

'Hey dad,' I said, lurching forward, 'Does this mean that Walker Enterprises will now become WalkerSithole Enterprises?'

Dad let out a short exaggerated 'ha-ha', releasing a brace of warm whiskey fumes all over the cab.

'No bloody chance!' he said.

75

I DIDN'T SLEEP WELL after all that. This cold quiver breezed over me when I thought of my evening with James. I was sure I'd said some things that had hurt him, cutting words which may now have this forward momentum, this other life they'd come to inhabit, especially if he'd gone and told his father and his father had taken offence. He was a strongman in the ruling party, capable of anything, the wrong family to piss off. The whole business deal could now be in jeopardy. Dad would be furious. I was stupid to goad James with glimpses of what was on my phone. I was aware the whole time this taut undercurrent had stifled the air, throwing sparks between us, my cruel way of inflicting on him the fact that meticulous collections of butterflies and expensive hats could never make up for what I knew he most wanted, to be a white kid like me. I lay there somehow sure I'd inflicted a severe wound, or that in various ways we all had on each other, what with Julius and his posh whiskey, Julia and her flute, various weapons being bared and thrust about, and now had this uneasy fear that through these wounds we'd somehow be forced to always share this deeper, darker connection.

FRIDAY. THERE WAS NO SIGN OF RESPITE. We laboured lazily through eight periods of school and in the afternoon, of all things, there was the commitment of a cricket fixture to play. We toiled on the field, our skins lathered in thick coatings of sunscreen lotion our mums insisted we plaster on us, our limp white cricket linens straining to keep out the blaze. At least our faces enjoyed some shelter under the stiff canopy of wide-brimmed hats, but our hair was mopped, slicked with sweat, our foreheads dribbling constant beading streams. Another bitch of an afternoon.

I said just this to Fruity in the slips.

'Jeez, tell me about it,' he said.

'What was that you said, Walker?' Mr Carrick asked, straining his neck at us, perched on his shooting-stick behind the stumps.

'Nothing sir,' I replied, and now I was thinking quickly. 'I was just saying to Peach that it's a hitch we can't seem to take a wicket.'

He glowered at me. The old fool wasn't as dumb as we took him for.

'Just play the game,' he said.

'Sir.'

We all shared a muffled giggle behind the stumps, even the sullen batsmen joined in.

OUR PARENTS RECLINED ON THE SIDE LINES, fanning themselves in the mottled shade of the broad fever trees. Businesses all across town had closed for the afternoon, Friday being any excuse for a liquid lunch, a boys' cricket match and a heatwave a handy added justification. There were chests of cooler boxes, dark blue, plastic red, grubby white lids lined up all along the rows of deck chairs. The dads glugged cold beers fished from brick cylinders of ice while the moms sipped glasses of chilled white wine, vodka coolers, gin and tonics or mild ciders with a slice of lemon wedged into the bottle neck. The women chattered and gossiped and we presumed they spoke of idle noth-ingness. The men talked rugby, business, maybe fishing, definitely the crappy state of the country.

We knew all this from the field even without hearing a word of it, being Friday afternoon during cricket season.

Our spinner Monty Dickenson skipped in from his short right-angled run up and tossed in a slow high-pitched off-spinner. The batsman took a stride forward, his eyes widening. His intention to whack it full toss was well signposted, but he missed, the ball curving past his pads plump into Kelinveldt's keeping gloves.

'How's that?' we all screamed, leaping up in the slip cordon with an explosive surge of energy. It rallied to the midfielders, even as far as poor Matthews on the boundary who distantly raised his hands a second later in flat bewildered hope. This was the most energetic the game had gotten in the last hour and a half.

'Not out,' Carrick said.

There were audible sighs. The deflation that rippled round us was brutal.

'Crap,' I said to Fruity.

THE MATCH PETERED OUT into a pointless draw and along with it my mood soured. It was going on five-thirty when the umpires finally met in the centre to call the whole farce off at the fall of a wicket. I sat slumped on the batsman's bench, disbelieving in the cruelties of the world, padded up to the nines, a clown clad all in white, as I had been for the last forty-five bloody minutes. I wanted to put my gloved hands to my face and scream. The pads had been so cumbersome I felt as if my legs were wrapped in a dozen layers of cotton wool and pinned up in front of a three filament heater. I didn't even have the energy to peel back the Velcro straps, bring about that instant release of tension to my shins, let the blood flow, though I did whip out the box from my sweaty, itchy crotch and slapped it down into my kit bag. It was in those moments that I thought I hated such a boring, stupid game.

MY MOOD DIDN'T GET BETTER in the car when Mom announced she had invited the Peach and Watson families over for a post-match *braai*. I particularly wanted to be alone, so much that I felt a wave of unbidden tears swell into my eyes. *Grow the hell up*, I thought, sitting forward, brushing away the filmy tiredness from my sun-swollen eyes. I refocused on the slip of grey road ahead, the crawl of Friday rush-hour traffic, and realised I had actually been levitating half in a desolate dream, featureless, sterile and somehow quite fearsome. I blinked a couple of times.

'What's that?' I asked.

'I said I've invited the Peaches and the Watsons over for a quick *braai* and a swim.'

'Oh cool, that's awesome,' I said.

WHEN WE ARRIVED HOME Becca's Fiat Uno was parked out in the drive.

'Must have plans,' Mom remarked.

'Must have,' Dad said.

It was just going on six, but Becca was already dressed up and preoccupied with messaging someone on her phone.

'Making plans?' Mom asked.

'Yes,' she said, 'we're going to Callie's for pre-dinner drinks if that's okay?'

'That's nice Beccs. And then?'

'Going to dinner, remember I told you. Ally's eighteenth.'

'Oh right. That's tonight?'

'It's tonight Mom, I've been telling you all week.'

'Just make sure you get a healthy dose of studying in tomorrow morning to make up please.'

'Yes mom!'

Dad lugged the cooler box through to the scullery and came into the hallway to hang up the car keys on the teak rack. I was labouring with my oversized cricket kit bag which I dumped in the hallway by the half-circular table that stood under a huge bronze framed mirror.

'Not there Danny,' Mom said.

'Mom!'

In the mirror I caught a glimpse of Dad's eyes as he performed a quick disapproving scan of Becca's outfit from top to toe.

The dress was indeed very short, black and satiny and stylish, extending just halfway down her supple thighs, and it was very well-fitting round her slender figure, her defined chest. It was not an uncommon outfit for a girl of eighteen to be wearing, but it didn't bother me then the way it seemed to bother my father.

A SHORT TIME LATER I was slumped in front of the TV, still in my sticky cricket whites, feeling lethargic. Mom was in the kitchen whipping together salads and meat in preparation for the *braai*. She told Petra to boil some potatoes, defrost a heap of meat in the microwave. Out on the veranda Dad was shovelling some coals, wood and firelighters into the grate. He rolled up sheets of old newspapers into balls, stuffed them into the pyre he was busy building. He had Ignatius there, handing him pieces of wood from the barrow he wheeled up to the veranda from the garbled pile behind the garage.

'No, not that one,' he said, 'smaller ones first.'

'Yes boss.'

I glanced over at them from time to time, a touch guilty because normally I was by his side helping when we had *braais* or when we did what we considered manly things about the house. I was dead beat, sunburnt and realised, searching for thin excuses, I had a dull, throbbing headache.

Becca came into the lounge, fussing with her keys, her phone, her small black handbag.

'Make sure there's money on your phone,' Mom called to her.

'Yes.'

'What time are you coming home?' Mom asked.

'I should be back by twelve.'

'Okay, no later. Remember, a fresh start for studying tomorrow. Take keys. We might be asleep by then.'

'With that lot coming over? I somehow doubt it. You'll be partying harder than I am.'

From opposite directions I heard my parents give out a knowing chortle, but I let out an involuntary groan from where I was sitting on the couch, my temples blistering in pain. I wondered what Matt would have to say about her needing to be home at that unfashionably early teenage hour. Would she sneak him in, or would he sneak her back to his place? Could they do it in his car? Or hers?

'DANNY, WHAT'S WRONG WITH YOU my boy?' Dad said from the veranda. I looked back at him, a tall fuzzy silhouette clutching a beer bottle against the frayed orange lateness of the sun. I scrunched my eyes up at him. They scratched and burned.

'Nothing,' I said, annoyed by this disruption to my solitary funk.

'You've been in this dozy, crappy mood all day.'

'I haven't.'

'Well you were hardly a bundle of energy out on the field were you?'

'Dad it was like forty degrees in the shade. Plus we had a late night last night. I'm just tired.'

'Yeah, but look Dan, you need to show you're up for this kind of challenge hey. It's what people notice. Especially as you're growing up fast now. You can't be making excuses like a kid forever.'

I breathed in deeply, knowing I had to keep the air tight in my lungs, let it out slowly, because if I exhaled I would only be letting on to my bratty indifference. Dad was looking at me, all that molten brightness crashing behind him. He took a long sip of his beer, the dark bottle stuck to his lips for an age.

'Okay?' he said.

'Yes dad.'

'Christ, bloody teenagers! Right my boy come and help me unpack the cooler box.'

BECCA LEFT, then our guests arrived in quick succession. The adults were out on the veranda talking a mountain of shit, drinking a gutful. Fruity, Watts and I kicked about in the pool a bit, hydrating our scorched red skin. We tossed a mini rugby ball about. The dogs leapt around the edges, tracking the ball as we threw it between us, yelping and squealing.

Dad stood over the *braai* cooking *boerwors*, marinated steaks, barbeque chicken kebabs. He stoked the meat till it flamed up on the red hot coals and when it did he was quick to douse it with a spattering of beer. A draft of hot smoke hissed and we all thought he was nuts standing over that inferno.

'Mad dogs and Englishmen, Dave,' Barry Watson said.

'Well I'm no bloody Englishman,' Dad replied.

We ate the meat with cool potato salad, coleslaw, garlic rolls charred in tinfoil. I didn't think I was very hungry, but munched away.

'Crikey child,' Mom said, leaning over the picnic table, planting her hand on my brow. 'You're practically crimson. Just feel how flushed you are.'

'They've all been well and truly *gotchered*,' Trudy Peach added, looking over at Fruity.

I waved Mom's hand away and carried on eating, moody again. Ever since getting out the pool I had been feeling this laziness drifting over me. My eyes were beginning to droop.

The men chatted a bit about business. God, here we go, I thought. Something more about the banks being a stuff up, the threat from the government to take over the white and foreign-owned companies, the problem with getting credit, them all agreeing it was better to try and hold what they called 'liquid cash'.

Dad slapped his hand on the table. 'Done and dusted on that score,' he said.

'Serious?' Mike Peach said.

Dad nodded. 'Did it Wednesday. Not taking any chances with this lot. I'm not leaving my cash with any bloody *munt* bank that's for sure. No, mine's all safely tucked away under the mattress thank you very much.'

I picked my ears up at this odd expression and wondered which mattress he was referring to. I supposed it must be their king size posturepedic. I wondered if it made it uncomfortable, whether they even noticed all that money stashed underneath it? I made the slimmest mental note to check it out, before realising my stupidity.

'Yeah, I'm sure the shit's about to hit the fan around here in a grand colossal way,' Barry Watson said.

'Yip. What's bloody new?' Dad said.

I was waiting for either him or Mom to give a report back on our eye-opening outing to the Sithole's, probably with all the usual embellishments highlighting the racial and cultural oddities we'd lapped up, but they didn't. Not even the bizarre display of those insane white cars all fiercely lit up behind all that glass warranted a mention. For some reason they appeared to want to keep news of the deal on the quiet, as if they were embarrassed by it, wanting to avoid it at all costs. By not mentioning it, I began to feel it was becoming part of the atmosphere anyway.

THEN SALLY WATSON flashed a broad smile at us boys, leant forward, resting her chin in her slender, creamy, diamond studded hands. Instinctively we all took fright, each feeling it surge through us, a trio of batteries all connected up together, looking out for one another's interests.

'So it's the dance coming up next week, guys,' she said. 'You all excited?'

We moaned collectively, but already sensed our obvious mistake.

'Oh yes,' said Mom, egged on, 'next Friday already.'

'You boys all got yourselves nice hot dates?' Trudy Peach asked. Now all the moms had their chins resting in their hands. They were leaning forward, looking at us, grinning in wide-eyed studied anticipation, a three-pronged attack.

'Mom!' said Fruity.

There was a chuckling chorus of womanly glee.

'Don't blush now boys. Come on. Tell us the low-down.'

'How can they not blush,' Barry Watson said, 'look at them, they're all suffering from third-degree burns.'

Laughter all round, the fraught awfulness of those edgy few moments at once dissipating smoothly through the gathering, and there was restored again the sense of comradely unity we all cherished, the inner ties that bound our shrinking community of whites, families coming together, feasting on a fatty braai, a near continuous flow of beer and white wine, loyal lazing dogs, the darkly restful pool beyond us and above a Friday summer night's distant dotted sprawl over deepest Africa.

Across all this I was looking intently at Mom, begging her with a fearful, pleading glare not to spill the beans about what had so far been our little secret, mother to son, about the unrivalled triumph of already securing the perfect date for our end of year junior high dance, the much sought after, the sweet, the beautiful Amy Whitaker.

AFTER THE BRAAI the three dads, three boys, three dogs played a bit of French cricket out on the lawn. The three moms sat nattering, nursing flutes of white wine.

'Oh yes, got to burn off all that *nyama*,' Barry said, lifting up his shirt to pat his globed beer-belly stomach after he half-heartedly lunged for the tennis ball Watts nicked in his direction.

'Christ, join the club,' Dad said.

The dads didn't have the stamina to last that long so after half an hour they surrendered to their beers, the game fizzling out. The three of us boys took a moment's delight in our victory, then slumped off into the house, to my bedroom where I quietly closed the door behind us.

'Do you have it?' Fruity asked.

'Yeah,' I said.

I had been waiting a good few weeks for this big reveal of mine, posting boasts and hints about it on our secret chat group every so often. Now the time had come, so I pulled out the tatty dog-eared copy of *Hustler* from under my pillow, the one I had secretly siphoned off from the stash I had come across at the back of Dad's cupboard, behind the heap of his winter pullovers and jerseys. Its glossy cover of a tanned bare-chested beauty with long wavy blonde hair, a seductive pout of dark pink lips, a gorgeous pair of firm, shapely boobs caught a momentary glint from my bedside

85

lamp and shimmered radiantly, intensifying my mates'
randy enthusiasm.

'Wow,' said Fruity.

He and Watson eagerly thumbed through the magazine
while I basked in the momentary triumph of my daring
brilliance.

'Look at the tits on this one,' Fruity said, holding it up for
us all to ogle at. We laughed.

'There's much better pussy online,' Watson said.

'Yeah but this old vintage stuff is class as well.'

'It's not bad.'

'Plus it has the added bonus of being available twenty-
four seven, if you know what I mean. No slow crappy
download speeds or when ZESA's out late at night and
your phone's fucking dead. What more could a guy want?'

'Hey, Walks,' Fruity said, 'I bet your sister has a great
pair of tits.'

'Hey,' I said. 'Fuck you.'

'And that firm arse,' Watson added, miming its shape
with his hands.

'Just watch it,' I said, landing a hard punch square on the
meat of his upper arm. 'That's my bloody sister!'

'Ow,' he yelled.

The three of us fell about my bed in a fit of laughter, mock
fighting. Then Fruity and Watts shot up, their eyes met,
widening in a merging stare, their intent menacing. They
darted out my room, trailing cackles of laughter with them.
Already I could hear them next door, in Becca's room,
shrieking, goading one another on. I went after them, but
Fruity had already peeled open the drawers in Becca's dressing table and had found what they were looking for.

'Check this out,' he said in an excited whisper, clawing at
a handful of Becca's bras and panties. He tossed a couple to

Watson and they threw them back and forth while I tried to leap up, snatching at the air. It was like playing piggy in the middle, as if we'd abandoned caution to our four year old selves again, except we all knew we weren't four years old, that this was skirting something far darker, openly puerile.

'Hey, cut it out, assholes,' I kept saying, but I knew how futile it became trying to stop my friends once they'd set out on a mission, the devil in them. After a while I fell exhausted to Becca's bed, laying there watching while Fruity held a pair of scant lacy panties to his crotch and made all too obvious thrusting movements towards them with his hips, while Watts fingered the outline of a breast in the firm cup of a bra, then made as if he were squeezing it. They both made stupid noises, imitating sex. I put my head back laughing, half appalled, pulling a pillow over my head, rolling my body around on my sister's bed.

WE MIGRATED TO THE LOUNGE where I loaded a game on the PlayStation and we sat about furiously fingering the controls, the easy instant pleasure of massacring hordes of gangsters, angular faced, grotesquely muscled, that loomed at us from the corners of some futuristic hellhole of a city's deserted streets and alleyways. The persistent stuttering pop of the caps we blasted endlessly into animated torsos and heads made us tire quickly.

The next thing, we were all heaped over the sofas, our lean bodies a muddled contortion of limbs, dozing and slumbering, our breaths fallen together into that deep unhindered rhythm that friends share, and Trudy Peach was standing over us saying to her husband that they'd better get their exhausted dead-to-the-world kid home.

NOW IT WAS QUITE LATE, around eleven-thirty. I'd fallen onto my bed in my white cricket shorts, still a touch damp from swimming. I was an inch from deep sleep, hearing only the muffled sounds of Mom and Dad locking up, the muted clinks clearing the empty glasses and plates from the veranda, the distant, dissolving joy of hearing them give the patient dogs their night-time biscuits. I succumbed to this delicious state of carefree abandonment, absolved from the bore of routines and chores, sensing everything was in perfect control about me, presided over by an older responsible force. I was both awake enough and tired enough to feel completely content.

THERE WAS A FUZZY PASSAGE OF TIME where I was lost in deep sleep, slipping only to the briefest awareness of turning on my side, causing the warm air to lumber about me, to curl, resettle against the clammy heat of my skin. Then I woke quite clearly, a sharpness pressing at my ears because I heard what sounded like a woman's stifled cry, not sure whether this was my mother or my sister. It was one of their voices, I had them locked down deep in my brain. It was a wordless half-grunt that I couldn't immediately uncouple, and it got me at once in the throat so I missed a breath and was sitting suddenly upright, gasping, feeling a little woozy, light-headed, the force of panic already rising through my still slackened body. I went rigid, momentarily, caught up in the confusion, but then the immediate lapse of time worked equally to dissolve everything around me, so just as quickly doubt slid over me, coaxing my body to relax again. I was about to lay my head back on the cool sleeve of my pillow when I heard Dad's heavy strides come thudding down the passage. My bedroom door was pulled closed, the key turned like a whip-crack and yanked out.

He hurried on, a panicked urgency in his footsteps. Already I had a vague understanding of being locked in my room for some reason, aware something was wrong, very wrong.

EVENTS ESCALATED RAPIDLY. I was sitting upright on the end of my bed, fully awake, listening to Dad repeat the same cold lead phrase over and over.

'No, there's *no* one else in the house, okay, there's *no* one.'

In the confusion I had turned my lamp on and was struggling to wade against the bright blinding shower of light towards the door. I was about to try open it when it occurred to me what Dad was saying. There's *no* one else in the house, *no* one. He was speaking in exaggerated, loud tones, and I was startled when the comprehension of what he was saying began to quicken within me, that he was trying to communicate a message to me to stay quiet, to stay still for my own damn good, to shut the bloody hell up.

I DUCKED DOWN, the rigid column of my body shot through with a stiffening fear, and I collapsed awkwardly to the floor, but at once I was crawling insect-like back to my bed. I don't know where this scurry of energy came from, some other automation had kicked in, because otherwise I felt the helpless drift of paralysis begin to waft over me from my feet upwards, some fast-acting venom pumping through my veins, turning my limbs and muscles to rubberised waste. I fumbled with the lamp switch, it was dark again. Rings of stippled broken light rolled about me, pulsing at my wide eyes, and then, sitting there at the lonely vortex of this darkness, I knew with certainty there was an alien presence in our house. Everything seemed immediately wrung in the grip of this malign, tensile sensation. Everything was hard, angular, hotly cold against my nerve-pinched flesh. My skin was tingling, I began to shiver. I brought my hand to my mouth to muffle my cries.

MY THOUGHTS RACED. What was happening seemed to take place in a series of unconnected scenes, each one mere seconds, fading in, fading out, my mind faltering to thread them to a logical sequence of events, to grapple towards some plausible, plastic meaning. I felt entrapped, convinced that every little unsighted thing was a threat. Everything remained a fractured blur, a long continuous shudder up the spine that unfolded on the curve of that moonless night. There was a murmuring, an unintelligible current of voices, movements that seemed to gyrate out at me, prod at my acidy nerves, but then there was also these long moments of the most oppressive silence imaginable.

A DISTINCT DULL CRACK, somewhere down the passage, maybe furniture, a wooden table toppling, followed by what sounded like the shuffling lumber of a scuffle. Mom shouted out. Her cries were muffled into a hand that came from behind her, compressed over her mouth. I didn't see this, but knew it had happened.

THEN PEOPLE WERE MOVING in different places. I sensed the presence of bodies come near, up the passage, about the hallway, in and out of the rooms, before they dissipated further away, the muttering falling to a distant contorted burble. I heard Dad pleading, his voice weighed down with this dead gravity. Yet it was also thin, lacking embodiment, as if some other purely mechanical personality had stepped in, taken control.

'Have whatever you want,' he said, 'it's all yours *shamwari*, but please just leave us alone.'

The intruders spoke in a mix of garbled English and Shona. I knew some Shona from school and from bantering back and forth with Petra, but I couldn't make out very much. I couldn't work out how many there were. This constant stream of aggression shifted from one to the other, as if they were passing round a gyro which they charged with threats, never allowing it to slow, the fright not diminishing for an instant.

I HEARD FOOTSTEPS come right past my door. I heard a jangle of keys, a thud of wood, a metallic echo. They were in Mom and Dad's room, opening the safe in their cupboard.

A PERIOD OF SILENCE. Then everything began to soften, dissolve into a puzzling void. I began to wonder whether it was now over, why Dad hadn't come to let me out. I crept a few paces closer to the door and listened. There was a muted sound somewhere, but it was vague, ordinary, an unvarying static hum across the breadth of the house, really no sound at all.

I WONDERED WHY the dogs weren't going mad, why Petra and Ignatius hadn't come to our rescue. I realised I had left my cell phone in the lounge so I couldn't even call the neighbours. I crawled close to the door summoning the nerve to place an eye to the keyhole. The passage light was bright, white, hard. I couldn't see much, except this stark infiniteness.

I waited for a long time, tempted to shout out, desperate to do something, anything, but the nerve failed me. I focused on the light in the passageway because it seemed a temporary soother from the dark, a tunnel which could connect me to my loved ones whose whereabouts I knew networked out from this pulsing space.

THEN A BLUE MASS crossed the keyhole. It was so close I could see the very texture of that blue, as if its coarseness rubbed against my eyeball. It startled me, I fell backwards. Then a warm liquid drenched my shorts, my bladder was failing. I cupped my hands to my crotch but the firm jet of urine funnelled through my fingers. I let it run.

I HID NEXT TO MY BED, a while later becoming aware of the electric gate being rolled along its coaster. I knew that jerky off-kilter rhythm. It halted with a loud slam, followed immediately by our dogs barking, then the sound of a car starting up, its accelerator pumped hard, doors being cranked shut, speeding off. The dogs soon died down to a whimper, then there was silence again.

I began to sweat. My legs stung where I'd pissed myself. I could feel cramps coming on. I sat panting on the carpet. It was only when I began to steady myself a bit I realised our attackers had fled. The tension that held everything had suddenly gone, vanished, and there was just this looming stillness, a plaintive, deadening calm.

I MOVED TOWARDS THE WINDOW, nervously parting the curtains, but I couldn't see much. The light was poor, the lone street lamp outside our yard was paltry, casting only a dull orangey pool of light over the road. It was enough for me to see the gate standing ajar. It brought me right back to the sound of its opening some moments before, to the understanding of the crystalline collaboration between sound and assumption. I figured that if I was right about the gate, I must have been right about every other detail I'd been piecing together. I saw those men, in my mind, the sound of their voices morphing into a figment of blue fabric and black skin I snatched from a keyhole. It all came together.

I RUSHED TO THE DOOR, hammering, yelling as loud as I could, but there was no response. I moved to the window, shouted for help, but my voice was small, high with terror and didn't carry far. Our yard was large, the neighbours' yards were large too. It was after midnight, everyone fast asleep. I thought of breaking the window with my cricket bat, but I was a quivering wreck and didn't have the guts to clamber out into the hostile nakedness of the night. Even the shudder of shattering glass would probably have failed to wake Petra and Ignatius, asleep at the far end of the property.

I shouted for help at the window. I bellowed and called, randomly, helplessly. I never expected it, but a man finally appeared in the driveway. I didn't see him until he was standing there, a statue, beside a bicycle, peering about the yard. I ducked below the windowsill, thinking it was one of the intruders who'd heard me yelling and come back. Then I realised it couldn't be. This man was stooped and old, a *madala* adrift late on a Friday night, just happening to saunter down our road when he walked into the middle of a crisis. Despite the hot night he was wearing a long grey trench coat, a wide brown bowler hat. He hovered there, squinting at me.

'Can you help me, please,' I shouted. 'Come here, come.'

He staggered up the driveway, his bicycle wobbling beside him. He was either drunk on *chibuku* or high on *mbanje*, but already I knew this *madala* was destined to be a saint that night, our unwitting, unlikely saviour.

I ASKED HIM to go call the Whitakers next door.

'Please *shamwari*, go to that house next to this one and call the owner, please. *Tstotsis* have robbed us.'

He didn't understand, so I used my shaky pigeon Shona as best I could. He leaned his bike against the wall and jogged off. I heard him thumbing on the gate of the Whitaker's place. Dogs down the road began to bark, our dogs joined in. Then he came back, clapping his hands, shrugging his shoulders.

'Okay, go around the back,' I told him, pointing, 'go to the domestic quarters, to the *kia,* and call the workers. Go quickly, *manya, manya!*'

Ages went by. I had edgy visions of the task this poor man faced, stumbling aimlessly round our yard, not knowing what he was doing, where he was going, lost in this maze of dark masses and shadows. The domestic quarters were hidden behind a thick, tall hedge at the far back of the property, behind the kitchen, the garages, neatly out of sight, out of earshot, just as Dad had wanted them.

Ignatius came stalking into sight round the house, trailed closely by Petra. He was holding a *panga* he used to dig with in the garden, wearing only a pair of shorts. I felt my insides surge, a new energy, a wash of relief. But then a thought wavered that maybe he'd quickly slipped off his blue gardener's overalls, that the same blue splurge I'd seen at the keyhole may now be lying in a heap on the floor of his room at the bottom of our garden.

'Petra,' I called.

'Mr Danny, what is it? What has happened?'

When I told her she began to wail, her body convulsing

94

in a crude, hysterical reaction.

'Don't stand there, come and help us!'

Ignatius was already inside. I heard him storm down the passage. I envisioned his strides, the *panga* gripped in his fists.

'Boss, boss,' he was calling.

A loud deep thud ricocheted through the house. Then the echoless clang of steel striking something hard, over and over.

I thought of Ignatius. I thought of his blue overalls. I thought of the *panga* he was holding. I thought of the way we all talked to him. The way Dad barked orders left and right, the way we had accused him of spying on Becca. I realised a dreadful possibility.

'Jesus,' I cried, 'Petra go and phone boss Whitaker, GO!'

SHE HOBBLED OFF, whimpering with fright. The rending continued, then the sound of wood splintering. I was thinking he was hacking my family to pieces, this man I'd known since I was eight but probably didn't really know at all. I was at my door again, pounding so hard I hurt both my wrists but I kept banging anyway. I just kept believing it was all an inside job, that he'd come back to finish us off.

IN THE MIDDLE of all this I heard my father's voice break through the mayhem.

'Oh Jesus, Jesus,' he was saying. He was gasping, breathless. I heard Mom crying.

'Mom!'

She came running down the passage calling for Becca.

'Mom, I'm here,' I said again. 'I'm here, are you okay?'

'Dan, it's all right, we're fine,' Dad shouted. 'Are you okay?'

'I'm locked in my room.'

'I'm coming,' he said, 'just wait.'

'Oh my God!' Mom screamed.

'What's going on?' I shouted.

Petra was wailing again too, screaming uncontrolla-bly, and Dad was telling them both to calm down, to shut the bloody hell up. Then I heard someone else crying, but this was a deep, guttural groan that cut right through everything, a low primal earth-trembling grumble.

Then Dad was yelling 'fuck', short and stuttered, repeat-edly, and Mom wouldn't stop crying.

By now the Whitakers were over and Monica Whitaker was talking very sternly.

'It's okay Jenny, it's okay,' she said. 'Everything's going to be okay. Now come with me.'

'I'll call the police,' Tom Whitaker said.

'Fuck!' Dad screamed again. There was something so genuinely demented in his voice that the shock of the word detached itself entirely from any real meaning. It was just a sound, an exterior expression.

'What's going on?' I called again. 'I'm locked in here.'

'Just wait damn it,' Dad said, 'I'm coming.'

'No, Dave,' Monica said, 'he can't see this. The kid's better off in there for now.'

'What!' I said.

'Tom, go get the car,' Monica said. 'We need to get to the trauma centre,'

'Trauma centre? What's happened?'

'Nothing sweetie,' she said. She was standing right outside my door now. 'Your sister's been through a trau-matic experience, okay, and she just needs a doctor to give her a tranquiliser to help her settle a bit, all right? Now we just need you to be patient and wait nicely for a few more minutes. Can you do that for us Dan?'

'Okay,' I said.

I heard Tom Whitaker come speeding in the gate, reversing his Mazda 6 all the way up to the front door. I raced to my window. Monica and Mom came out on either side of Becca. They were holding her up. She looked weak and could barely walk, she was limping, hobbling as if her legs were just two long planks with no knee joints. She was wearing a long pink gown which I didn't recognise, but it hung slack off her shoulders, over the straps of that short black dress she went out in earlier. Her hair was a mop of wild dishevelment hanging down in strands, obscuring her face completely. They helped her into the back and Mom sat next to her, drawing her towards her. Monica climbed into the passenger's seat, then seemed to realise something so Tom got out of the driver's seat and Monica took his place, speeding off. Tom said something to Dad and ran out the gate, back home. It all happened too quickly for me to take in, yet at the same time that brief, graphic scene is one of the things that has stayed with me the longest.

'DAD,' I CALLED AGAIN.

'Okay, okay, I'm coming.'

Dad's voice sounded hard, gravelly, but a bit calmer. He was pacing up and down the passage.

'I don't know what I've done with the fucking key!'

'Hurry Dad.'

'I can't find the bloody key Dan, so just cool it.'

I crouched down, felt my brow. The sweat flicked off as I brushed my fingers over it. I was still in total darkness, I don't know why I hadn't thought to turn the lights on yet. At last I heard Dad at the door trying to insert the key into the lock but I could tell his hand was shaking. The key rattled, scratched at the varnished wood of the door. He was breathing heavily too, and sniffling.

'It's okay Dad,' I said, 'just take it easy.'

The door opened, a tunnel of light from the passage flooded the room. It was here now, the light, and I buried myself in my father's arms, sobbing like a baby.

Rebecca didn't come back, or Mom, or Monica Whitaker. The Stavrous and the Bells from down the road came. No one called the Moyos who lived next door to us on the other side, even though Mr Moyo was actually a specialist doctor and it might have occurred to us that it would have been quicker to ask him to administer a sedative to Becca.

The rest of the night Dad went through the whole procedure with the police, who Nicko Stavrou had gone to fetch. He and Travis Bell helped Dad with all the endless red tape. It seemed needlessly trying. Dad was exhausted, his patience severely tested when it came to dealing with the dim witted policeman. He was constantly on the verge of clapping him a shot around the earhole, but Travis Bell kept urging him to take it easy. I didn't hear what went into the statement Dad made to the police as Travis took Dad aside to the kitchen to write it while Maria Stavrou occupied me in the lounge. We had coffee and biscuits. Petra kept the kettle topped up. She fretted round us offering us another cup every five minutes. I felt a bit nauseas, my mouth dry, rubbery.

When I looked around the TV lounge it seemed as if nothing had been touched. The TV and DVD player were still on their stand, the stereo still setup by the wall. My phone had been where I'd left it, on the coffee table. In the dining room the silver was neatly stacked in the display cabinet. It was astonishing. The dogs were all fine too, locked up all the time in the courtyard. In my bedside drawer, hidden away behind some clutter, I had an old cigar box my granddad had given me. It held my own life savings, pocket money, birthday money, the grand sum of about seventy dollars. I knew that was safe too, so everything was fine.

It seemed as if we'd had a lucky escape.

ONE OF THE POLICEMEN came into the hallway asking to use the phone. 'Incident at Alice Smith,' he reported, 'No. 11, code six.' Then he explained, to either Dad or Travis or Nicko, that he'd sent for Special Crimes Branch, that this case required special attention.

A SULTRY, DEADPAN HOUR PASSED. All the doors, the windows were bolted closed, the heavy clad curtains adding to the tightness of the air, of being closed in. I couldn't now comprehend it any other way. I couldn't imagine the French doors ever again adrift to the unseen night, the wide open expanses of the garden, now that it had been complicit in harbouring our assailants.

The dull smell of dried urine about me, like a post-shock spoor, acted as something of a strange pacifier, but there was a faint sting prickling over my legs and I was too afraid to walk down the passage alone to the bathroom to wash myself, but too embarrassed to ask Maria Stavrou to come with me. I sat sipping coffee, absently watching the relay of a cricket match on TV while Maria occasionally rubbed my shoulders, patting me on the back, whispering comforting clichés close in my ears.

THE POLICE WERE STILL MILLING about the house. Their footsteps up and down the passage, clad in heavy boots, sounded both assuring and disconcerting. Apart from stomping around, they appeared to be doing very little. Dad was growing more impatient with them all the time. When they came into sight, he was trailing after them, steady-eyed, anxious, the tension stacked right through his body, though his head seemed angled downwards, too, now and again he lolled it or rolled it tiredly on his stiff neck, stretching out that fulsome jugular pressure of a nightmare come true.

THE GATE BELL RANG. I didn't react this time, there was just this condensed ether of dead, spent tranquillity, nothing spilling now, acid-like, down on the coursing network of my nerves. Or else I was just too bone-dead beat to respond, the exhaustion numbing me through.

Dad answered. 'Okay.'

The gates began to roll. I could hear from the lounge its cantered jerky screeching along the track. This did alarm me a bit. I didn't want those gates opening up a stark gaping porthole into our yard, allowing other strangers such easy passage. Faint headlights washed the screen of curtains, back-lighting them a weak white flush, then a fluid motorised sound swarmed up the drive, pulling to an abrupt halt. I heard a door opening, crisp on the outside night.

Dad unlocked the front door. 'Evening,' he said.

'Special Branch,' a man announced.

He came into half view in the hall. He wasn't wearing a uniform like the other cops, but black faded jeans, a red tight-fitting T-shirt, rather swanky brown suede leather boots, so blatantly irregular they stirred in me something curious, cautioning, an absurd anachronism years before

I would even know what an anachronism is. At once he started issuing instructions to his subordinates. They picked up their heels, energised themselves just a little. I saw him usher Dad into the kitchen.

FINALLY RESTLESS OF MY KEEPER, I fled Maria Stavrou's clutches, pacing myself tentatively towards the dining room. The large empty starkness of this space inhibited my movement, pinning me to the carpet, the impenetrable thickness of the navy blue curtains was what alarmed me, their slack concealment of what or who might be streaming across the window that very instant, figures and figments in that weltering outer dark. I was close enough to the kitchen to hear Dad answering the man from Special Branch's questions. Unlike the other cops before him, this one was eager, alert, his body fidgety, standing almost on tiptoes as if he was ready to dash out at any edgy second.

'They took your cell phones? If so we can trace them. What are the numbers? We can get these men, we can, but they are already halfway to the border, I can assure you of that. If we go after them we are going all the way, there is no turning back, there is no saying where this will all end tonight.'

'Okay,' Dad said, 'well can you do that, go after them?'

'Yes, but the only problem is petrol. I'll need petrol to chase them all that way.'

'I've got some spare,' said Tony Whitaker, 'in my garage, next door.'

'No it's better you give me cash. It's quicker to stop at a station and refill than decant from a container.'

'Yeah, okay,' said Tony. 'I've got cash in the car. Come, I'll get it for you.'

'Plus we'll need some *bonsellas* for the border officials.

These *tsotsis* have deals going with the customs officers, a share of the value of whatever merchandise has been stolen in return for issuing customs clearance. It's how they get hot property out the country. The trick is to offer them more. It may cost a bit, but at least we'll get your intruders.'

'Oh right,' said Tony. 'Yes, okay, I'll give you whatever cash we can get together.'

'Thanks Tony,' Dad said.

'Good. These bloody *tsotsis*,' the top cop said. 'Don't worry, their run is coming to an end. Justice is waiting for them. That's what I'm going to be bringing to them. This is what I do.'

'Okay,' Dad said.

'Good. Now here is my cell number, you can get an update from me on this.'

BY THE TIME DAD FINISHED with the police and everyone had gone, it was about four-thirty in the morning. Already the sky was thinning, there was a trace of liquid gunmetal in the air. It was strange to be up at that time – in the aftermath of what had happened everything was a touch unreal. Dad locked up, took me with him to the room. The door to the dressing room had been smashed in, splintered wood lay everywhere, ugly and spiky. I pieced its demise together, concluding that Ignatius must have bashed it in with the *panga* to set Mom and Dad free.

'Pretty bloody mess, isn't it?' Dad said.

He sat me on the end of the bed, putting his arm round my shoulders. Slowly he began to talk me though exactly what happened, just so I was clear about everything. It was hard to take it all in, his words were muddled, heavy, and I was woozy, my mind skirting the fringes of another world altogether, but when he mentioned aggressive intruders armed with revolvers, vicious threats, demands to be taken to the safe, I remained conscious enough to pay attention.

'They *kifed* all the money, the cash I'd taken out the bank,' he said.

'No ways,' I said.

'Yeah. And your Mom's jewellery, all her valuables, all stuff they could easily carry.'

'Jeez.'

'Had these satchels, stuffed all they could in those.'

'Is that all they took?' I asked.

I could see Dad had been under huge strain. He was contemplating the whole event, it was playing on a reel in his mind.

'Yeah,' he said, 'that's all they took.'

We sat there side by side for a minute or so. Dad was breathing heavily again, his chest labouring visibly, in and out. I wondered whether he was about to be sick.

'They brought your Mom and me into the dressing room,' he said, 'and tied us up with a handful of my ties before locking us in.'

I noticed how Dad had been gently rubbing his left wrist, a raw red ring round it.

'We were both gagged, pretty tightly. Couldn't do anything about it, pretty damn helpless.'

I asked where Becca was the whole time.

'Becca,' Dad said, 'well she was taken to her room and tied up too. Look, Dan, she's had a really scary night, okay, it's been bloody awful for her and as a result she's in a hell of a state. I just think it's better if none of this is spoken about, okay?'

'Sure Dad.'

'So let's be tough and put on a brave face for when your mom and sister come back, okay boy?'

'Of course.' Then I asked, 'Ignatius? He wasn't involved was he? I saw someone pass by the keyhole and I thought they were wearing blue overalls, like the kind he wears in the garden.'

'No, he wasn't involved. But you're right, come to think of it, they were wearing blue, all three of them were. Blue overalls and dish cloths tied round their faces. Couldn't see anything but black hands and those bloody black and white eyes.'

'Oh right,' I said, 'shit.'

This just slipped right out, falling off my tongue, but I knew that Dad wasn't going to clip me one over the earhole and chide me for using the s-word. It was clear we were passed all that now.

'Yeah,' he said, 'it's shit alright.'

Then something quickened in me, an internal shriek of fright, but sitting next to Dad I didn't mention that in a sketchy corner of my mind I saw the blurred shape of three men, three strange men in blue, sauntering down the hill behind me, trailing me as I had made my way home.

WE WASHED UP A BIT and then lay down next to one another. Dawn was breaking, of all things there was distinctive birdsong coming from the hedges, aflutter in the trees. Sweet fluty tweeting, the furious rustling of the leaves, the shrubs. I was exhausted, my eyes heavy. Neither of us slept. Dad kept stirring at every little sound and I knew he was awake beside me, his eyes fixed like steel on all that hard space about the room.

WHEN THE SUN WAS UP I slipped off the bed, walked down the passage. Now it had passed, all the adrenaline coursing through my veins waning, I could smell the presence of the intruders throughout the house. There was a distinctive sour smell about everything, a heavy acrid scent. I want to say it reeked of something stale and heady, like wood smoke maybe, but that can't be right. There was this stench of filth squatting in my nose, not real actual filth, but an association of what I now assumed filth and scum to smell like. I wondered whether we'd ever get that reek out the house.

I found myself in Becca's room, the odour drawing me there. Her lamp was still on. The bedspread ruffled. Draped over the gilded brass bars of her bed were two of Dad's ties, one on either end. One was plain black with a single white stripe across it, the other was a green tie embroidered with a gold emblem. I stared at them, cataloguing them in my memory. There was a third tie strewn at the foot of the bed. Then a fourth, this one still tied in a knot, lying just off the pillows. I could picture the way it must've sat across her mouth, tightly, gagging her cries, her shouts. I picked it up, ran my fingers over it. It was dry now, but I reckoned it must've been wet with her saliva where she'd tried to scream, call for help.

I felt sorry for my sister, picturing her tied up like that. She was only eighteen, I was only thirteen. A coagulated sense of trauma became comprehensible to me, as if standing over myself and Becca, looking down on us, wanting to cast a quilt over us, a veil of protection from this dense chaos I could envision coming towards us, awaiting us now. I was petrified every second I was locked in the dark, but Becca had a far worse experience than me. Staring down on her bed, the outline of a grim understanding came to me that something awful had happened to her, some unimaginable violation, but I couldn't allow myself to continue with the thought. I told myself I was going to make an effort to be extra nice to her when she came home.

A SHORT WHILE LATER, Dr and Mrs Moyo came round. Mrs Moyo took me aside, enveloping me in her hefty arms, her wide bosom, hugging me tightly for what seemed an age. Then she spoke to me very quietly.

'Oh Danny, you've been such a brave boy, haven't you?' she said. 'Such a big brave boy and you've been so strong! My, my, what a strong young man you are!'

She slipped her hand in her handbag producing a large slab of Nestle double-decker chocolate. She hugged me again as I began to sob, silently, gently against her fresh floral perfumed dress. There was this strange grandmotherly beauty and warmth in her soft, dark chocolate brown, gracefully aged skin. Somehow I recognised that. Her sympathy for me had depth, truth, and I needed that embrace so much right then.

'There, there,' she said, 'it's over now you brave young man.'

I was crying because I could already predict she was the only person who would do anything like that for me, I didn't think anyone else would ever say a word about it. I had been locked in my bedroom so everyone would assume I'd been spared the ordeal. The realisation of this terrified me in ways I couldn't justify or calibrate. I bet myself that no one would even bother to say well done to me, or say thank you for calling that old drifting *madala* to our rescue.

Only elegant Mrs Moyo. I could picture myself remembering that this act of kindness would sit with me for a long while. There was going to be so much happening now I knew I'd be the least of anyone's concern. But Mrs Moyo had heard the part I played, pieced together glimpses of my own ordeal, my own trauma hankered down in that dark enclosure, an eyeball on the end of a fraught, galvanised nerve-ending, looking out on a snatch of evil.

IN THE LOUNGE Petra had made yet more tea and coffee, this time boiling the water on the gas stove because the power had gone off. It seemed to take an age. We sat there, the Moyos and us. It was quiet in the house, long silences between speaking, no background prattle from the TV to cover the uncomfortable gaps. Dad was being polite, but his mind was a million miles away.

'This country,' Dr Moyo said, 'what has become of us? This type of thing is emblematic of the violent crime that has riddled places like Johannesburg and Durban, where gangs maraud and don't hesitate to draw knifes and fire revolvers at will. It certainly never used to be a scourge here, we've always been a disciplined people, a passive people.'

'Yeah,' Dad said, 'that's true.'

'Peter,' Mrs Moyo said, 'don't forget, people are desperate. It's a sign of desperation.'

'Petunia, my dear, the dire state of this once great country of ours doesn't excuse what's happened here one little bit does it? Nothing can ever justify *that*.'

Mrs Moyo shot an appalled look at me, then at Dad.

'No, no, I'm sorry,' she said, 'please forgive me, please! I never meant that for an instant.'

SHORTLY AFTER THE MOYOS LEFT I saw Dad going down to the *kia* and about an hour later Ignatius appeared with bundles of his belongings, stacking them at the gate. He stood about, or paced, lanky, panic-stricken. I was tired and not very focused, but the next time I looked, he was gone. I didn't ask Dad why he fired Ignatius, what reason he gave or what his thinking was, but our ex-gardener was never spoken of again.

I DIDN'T KNOW WHERE my mother and sister were. All Dad told me was that they'd stayed at my Aunty Jackie and Uncle Rob's place for the night because they were suffering shock. At ten he said we were going for a drive. We jumped in the Hilux, heading for town, towards Dad's offices. We trolled up palm-lined Samora Machel Avenue, then turned into Glenara. The wide green-paved frontage of the large suburban properties began to thin out to short patches of bare brown soil, sallow stalks of grass, flightless trampled litter.

The buildings got taller, squatter, greyer before trimming out to the flat industrial straggle of Graniteside. We didn't go straight at Coke Corner up to Dad's warehouses at Walker Enterprises, but took a right, cruising Workington Street before veering into a small shopping complex. There were hardware stores, construction merchants, takeaways. We pulled up outside a smart glass-fronted building, painted two stark shades of blue, pale and dark, signed JVS BANK in lean corporate letters.

'Wait here,' Dad said.

He was gone a while. It was hot in the car. He'd taken the keys, the windows were electric. I opened the door slightly to let the turgid mid-morning air edge inwards. I rested my head on the headrest, the heavy duty upholstery warm to the nape of my neck, my eyes drooping over in an unremembered moment. The last diluting milligram of fright syringed into my system was weakening, suppressed by an overwhelming exhaustion drifting me off to sleep.

Seconds later I woke to this flash of blue flanking my left side. A blue slither of movement and already I was pawing towards the driver's seat, across the hard handbrake, the gear-stick, when I realised the passenger door was open, leaving me vulnerable to this figure standing in blue overalls beside the car. I scrabbled forward, yanking the door shut, my mind spooling and faltering.

'Go away,' I yelled, 'go away, go!'

It's only a hawker selling brooms! I told myself, deconstructing my amped palpitations, chill the hell down. I decided it was just an innocent factory worker turned street vendor in his tea break, pawning homemade brooms to earn his buns and Coke. Still my chest swelled tightly, these stark horrors ballooning until it hurt. He was looking in at me with a displaced frown, my overreaction angering him, scuttling in him that ever-present edginess. When he raised a stubby finger to tap at the window I imagined he was going to smash the glass with the shaft end of the broom, reach in to sort this racist little white kid out, this British *murungu*. A second or two later he'd shrugged me off as a hopeless non-taker, sauntering on. Only then did I dare to breathe.

WHEN DAD GOT BACK I had relaxed. There were men in blue overalls all over the shopping complex, it turned out. I had been staring at them, fixated, numb. This fucking figures! I kept thinking. I was sweating, felt flushed but told myself this was only the heat of the morning, the distant impartial punishment of the sun. Dad was looking red-faced, flustered too. He closed the door abruptly, reversed hard. We took off, the V8 engine kicking off the tarmac with a brief ecstatic squeal.

Dad didn't say much but while we were streaming back up Glenara he looked over at me, then ran his clammy left hand across my hot sweaty brow.

'You okay Danny?' he asked.

'I'm fine, Dad,' I said.

BEFORE HEADING HOME we made one more stop, this time at Sam Levy's Shopping Village. We walked along the plaza, past various poky expensive shops on either side, the red brick façades of the buildings and pathways absorbing some of the steep late morning light, but still I felt it refracting off the wide glass frontages and seeming to wash back over me, spotlighting me there amongst the dozens of indolent Saturday shoppers. There was the odd familiar face that coasted towards us, one or two peers from school, a chatty bevy of girls. I was aware, today more than any other, of feeling hyper self-conscious, certain everyone was drawn to looking at me. I hadn't given much thought to my appearance, whether I'd brushed my hair, what I'd chosen to wear. I wasn't even wearing shoes, my bare feet tramping the roughcast brick and concrete. I was embarrassed to think that somehow my inward state of frazzled shock, my shaking limbs, chattering jaw, leaky bladder, was being broadcast to everyone, this shame signposted round my neck. I kept my head down, averting my gaze from the inquisition I was convinced was being levelled at me, walking on the inside of Dad, slinking along under the shadowed canvas overhangs of the shop fronts.

Dad led us into a retailer which said 'MURRAY'S JEWELLERS' in a discreet gold sign on the window. We were buzzed through a security grid, into the glorious instant skin-thrill of a small air-conditioned chamber, lushly carpeted against my tender feet. The ceiling-to-floor glass cabinetry, backed and surfaced with mirrors, distorted the sense of space, enhancing this cool dazzle of gold and silver.

'I'd like to buy a wedding ring,' Dad said to the suited, well-groomed black man who greeted us.

'Certainly, sir. Any specific preferences? Let me show

you what we have. Right over here if you please.'

'Just a plain gold wedding band, thanks,' Dad said.

AT NOON, Aunty Jackie and Mom arrived home. I hadn't seen Mom since before the robbery and ran out to meet her. She looked ashen and pale, without make-up. Even though I had seen her without make-up countless times, I was startled by how drawn and plain she looked in the bright stark November sunlight. There was no trace of colour in her at all, her features had withdrawn into her skin, so deeply she looked like an old expressionless doll. She didn't have any jewellery on either I noticed, making her look like a victim, the evidence of what they'd stripped from her. The burglary now became tangible, its effects and consequences real, even though I knew the reason she wasn't wearing jewellery.

I could appreciate she was tired but was still shocked by her attitude. It seemed so distant. She gave me a hug, but it was loose, non-committal. Mrs Moyo's hug was far better, more comforting.

'Okay Danny,' she whispered, 'I'm here now my boy.'

I could tell her mind was drifting, an age and a day away, so I never allowed myself to get very upset by this, as unfathomable as it was.

AUNTY JACKS AND MOM set to work right away. They stripped Becca's bed. Mom gathered all the linen, dumping it in Petra's arms.

'Burn these,' she said. 'Everything.'

They began moving all the furniture. Everything was rearranged, completely opposite to how it had been. I hovered in the passage, my stomach tight and sore, watching them fidgeting about. I sensed what they were trying to do, but the sheer force of the energy they undertook this operation with suggested something far more too, some cleansing process for their own sake. They put out bowls of dried flowers, the immediate heady scent of lavender and vanilla lifted into the room. They sprayed a sweet smelling aerosol all down the curtains, along the carpet, over the furniture. They put a huge hamper of fruit on the dresser, heaps of freshly cut, bright cellophane wrapped flowers in vases next to her bed.

'What are you doing?' I eventually asked, taking a nervous step into the room.

Aunt Jacks turned, forcing a smile in my direction.

'Nothing my boy,' she said, 'we're just making Becc's room nice for her for when she comes back, that's all.'

'Danny,' Mom said, 'go and see what your father's up to.'

IN THE EARLY AFTERNOON Mom and Aunty Jacks went off again. Dad came to find me. I'd been pacing about the house, in and out the lounge, up and down the passage. Out in the garden, I was traipsing along the driveway, looking at the black truncated fixture of our electric gate from slightly different approaches, from the front door, from the garages, from the brick pathway leading round the back of the kitchen, from the snaking slate-stone trail to the pool. I kept seeing flashes of a trio scaling the wall, or slinking in the gate. I kept wondering exactly how they did it, the secrecy and mystery of the whole affair part of its assault on us too, a larger grievous insult to our suburban pride and integrity.

'Danny,' Dad said, standing at the front door, 'put your tennis kit on. We're going to the club to have a set or two.'

'Really?' I said, 'what about Mom and Becca?'

'Your mom's with Becca now. But they'll only be back later on.'

'You sure we can leave?'

'Yes, come on, let's not mope around here, hey. There's nothing we can bloody do here.'

I scrambled to my room, donned my navy blue collared Nike shirt, my New Balance tennis shoes. I scooped up my bag of Babolats from the bottom of my cupboard and we headed out the door. He didn't say a word on the way, but when we got there news had travelled ahead of us. Everyone was quick to come over to offer their best wishes. Some of the old ladies gripped Dad's hands in theirs quite firmly, looked up at him, shook their heads, maternal and caring. He quietly thanked every one of them, whispering to them through a clenched jaw, and I thought that we had really come for this, what Dad had needed all day long, after his night of torment.

'This never would have happened back in the day ...' one of the older male members began to say, but Dad was quick to cut him off.

'Right, we've come to play some tennis,' he said, 'let's get a four going.'

Then I noticed the Whitakers coming in the gate. A little secret was that Amy and I played at the same club. This meant I had exclusive access to her most Saturday afternoons, the two of us youngsters amidst a sea of elders, something I was keen to keep from my over eager friends, at least until I showed her off as my date at our end of year junior dance. I saw her, at once rushing over, someone young and pretty to lose myself with for a time.

'Hey Amz,' I said.

'Hi Danny, how are you? I'm so sorry about what happened.'

WE PLAYED TWO SETS EACH and I got to chat with Amy a bit before Dad said we needed to be heading home again. In the blistering white hot heat of the day Dad was flushed red and sweaty, but he seemed cooler, less rigid. Finally, later in the afternoon, Rebecca returned home. I was lectured on how I was not to say anything to her about the ordeal, I was not to ask upsetting questions. She was fragile, they told me, she needed peace and rest.

'It's tough for women after these things,' Dad said, as if that clarified everything as a brother, a son, a boy jolted somehow onto the cusp of manhood by the events of a single, unfathomable night.

I gave my assurances, for some reason buying into the secrecy of the whole scheme absolutely. They had already decided the best way to deal with Becca was to strip away all mention of what had occurred to her, as if details and a name given to her experience would only hamper her recovery. Or else I suspected they had formed a secret trio, deciding from now on to exclude me from all information. As I was just a boy, as I hadn't been part of the actual attack, locked away in the dark, useless, petrified and pissing myself stupid, they may have thought it best if I stayed oblivious to everything.

Aunty Jacks and Uncle Rob drove her home. Mom was in the back seat with her and Becca never said anything when she got out the car. She'd been crying constantly, her eyes were red and bloated. She whimpered as she came past but never acknowledged me. There was something about her, the way her body moved now, heavy-footed, rigid, that as a dancer startled me. Deep down this served to fortify my formless suspicions of an act which I still couldn't bring myself to contemplate. I couldn't get to grips with anything, couldn't grasp the gravity of it. Nothing was holding. Everything was loose, shifting, like sands of the desert. It seemed unreal and impossible, so I decided to go about my own business for the rest of that sullen weekend. I would dip my feet back into my childhood, the wonder years of carefree abandonment, the fantastic failure of meaning, the flights and fancies of an imagined world.

Aunty Jackie had bags with her. She was moving into the spare room. Between her and Mom, it was already apparent that an almost constant vigil would be held at the side of my silent sister's bed.

THE POLICE CAME BACK early Sunday morning. They looked outside, rummaging in the shrubs, the hedges, scouting the wall for footmarks. They were making notes. One of them had a camera, though I never saw her take any pictures. I listened out for news of the top cop from Special Branch, whether he'd caught up with our crooks at the border, when he was going to return all of Dad's money, Mom's jewels, but nothing was mentioned of him and I don't think Dad bothered to ask. Then they came inside, Dad showing them again where the intruders had been, what they touched. They dusted for finger prints on the safe, in the dressing room. They wanted to dust for prints in Becca's room too but Mom shouted at them to stay the hell out. I slunk around trying to avoid them, fearful that when they had no more prints to dust for or no leads to follow up, they'd begin to ask me questions. I would have to tell them about the three men in blue overalls who may or may not have followed me home on Tuesday after my pranks at the bottle store. I'd have to tell them why they may have followed me. I might be arrested for pissing on the President's face. What would happen to a skinny white kid in jail? They didn't ask anything, not seeming to know

I existed, so that remained my little secret, hidden deep down in my beating breast.

LATE SUNDAY AFTERNOON the heat-wave finally broke, the clouds loured in, then small crystalline drops of rain started to fall in an instance of wonder which became heavier, harder, intensified until there was a brisk, brief pelting shower which afterwards left the driveway and the surrounds of the pool delivering up to the air wafts of steam, the smoky aftermath of a great tectonic rift in the earth. Despite being the first mystic rainfall of the season none of my family commented or revelled in the instant relief from the heat it granted. Only I ran out, forcing myself to dance a small improvised jig in the runny puddles, skid over the wet spongy lawn.

2

THE RAIN CAME AGAIN later that night, a brief, quick drenching, further release from the domed pressure building over us. Sheets of water fell from a barrel-black sky, nailing the ground in rods, hammering down in steel strips across the dull splay of the single bulb wired to the corner of the veranda. Stupidly, standing at the locked French doors, peering out the curtain to the glassy blackness, I convinced myself that the rain, the churning sky, the distant rumble, was all one grand atmospheric gesture of commiseration for our misfortune. But it was bullshit. I came away, the curtain falling into the shape of the space I left, closing the outside off for a long time, perhaps permanently, so now it was just us, insulated in that insulating space.

Dad was pacing about, a fixed agitation cast about him as if his insides had been caught in a net and he was writhing about in the dark murk to break free, but couldn't. His body was acting as a passive barrier, trailing him about, silent, pensive, on edge, though he was screaming and drowning too, floundering from the inside out.

He spent part of the morning knocking about an old trunk in the garage finding an array of padlocks. He wiped a decade's grunge off four of the biggest, ran the nozzle of a tin can of machine lube across their grooves and key slots, working them until the springs reloaded, the mechanisms wound back to life. The biggest one was looped and snapped through the wrought iron gate that closed over our front door, the door itself shut and locked. The others sat, armed and bronzed, on the dining room table awaiting commission. I knew the iron gridded bars were coming for the veranda, the scullery, Mom and Dad's sliding door from their bedroom to the pool. It was a matter of time. A phone was going to ring the following morning in a supplier's sales room somewhere in the industrial sites, my father telling them to send round their team, on the double, to measure up and fit their strongest security gates. His tone would be heavy and dry, not a voice haggling over prices. He would feel he needed to pay, pay whatever it cost, so afterwards other phones would start ringing in other businesses, alarm companies, security firms, fumigation services.

I CAME AWAY FROM THE CURTAIN, knowing I'd been looking out one last time on the openness of our garden, my heels dragging as if dumbbells were tied to them. Through the lounge I lugged my heavy self along the ceramic tiles, over the fine rugs in the hallway, onto the thick carpets of the passage where I stopped outside the half-closed door to my sister's room. I stood, standing, swaying. Absent-mindedly I'd been there three or four times already that evening, appearing, disappearing, stooping in, slouching off, making my meaningless arrival from different entry ways the simple configurations of the house offered. I had been coming and going like this before that second shower of rain drew me away to watch it fall into the outside dark, a brief, rootless distraction.

My sister, my mother, my aunt, this great unmovable outcrop around which the house had been built. Or these three bonded presences, strained, anxious, sightless to me behind the white gloss slab of the door. They had become soundless too, just occasional murmurs carried outwards, whispered undertones, as if anything uttered beyond a decibel would carry outwards signalling our weakness, our wounded family. I imagined them sitting there, heavy, deadpan, still for the longest minutes, only an odd shuffle to break the stoniness, the occasional toss of a head or a limb to shake their brooding, faltering minds. I stood, hovered, hearing nothing.

I MOVED OFF FROM THE DOOR, this time feeling heavier, more lethargic. Everything had seemed to stand still, stop functioning. My routine had been shattered and a bit later Dad insisted I come sleep next to him. I was tired and didn't raise any objections, feeling myself drift as I plodded along to my parent's room, stripping the shirt off my rain-dried torso, peeling down my shorts, chucking myself onto Mom's side of the bed in only my underwear. No one checked whether I'd bathed or not, my feet near clad black with muck, or whether I had brushed my scummy teeth. I just let my head fall to the pillow, smelling my mother there, some small mercies still left in my world.

It was awful. Dad refused to put the overhead fan on, muttering about the whipping of the blades drowning out any intruder. We lay there side by side, hot and sweaty, his large bulk disconcerting to me, something unnatural now that this was the first time I'd slept by my father's side since I was a toddler basking in his heavy breath, my head nestled in the nook of his thick clammy arms. His deep inhalations were longer and stronger than mine and I wanted to one day be a man just like him, big, burly, in control of everything around him. Now I lay turned away from him, this long adult shape, my legs tucked up, my hands discreetly cupped over my regular night-time erection, strengthening and weakening, smattering me with embarrassment, an inkling I should feel ashamed, disgraced it had come on this night of all, but I didn't somehow, not yet.

The mosquitoes buzzed, unseen, feasting off us. We tossed and turned, slapping ourselves stupid to be rid of them, but it seldom worked. We scratched robotically at our bites and at the smallest sound, Dad was up, a stiff tall shape, his jittery nerves casting his senses about the house, his mind's eye concocting visions of predators snooping the outer walls of our home. Dead into the night I was miserable, too afraid to whimper, to make the smallest sound or movement. It was all inside, vacuum packed, held in. I didn't know it was possible to be thirteen and carefree one moment, never doubting a thing about life, enjoying the freedoms of a blissful childhood, and then to be overwhelmed by a sudden oppressive force which had no name, no physical attribute, but was rather a state of mind. When dawn broke at the curtains I had barely slept, though the sheer relief of lying through that fraught, nervy night was the only energy that dripped through me, enough for me to get up, carry on.

UNLIKE BECCA, I was made to return to school almost at once. Monday morning I was tugging on my school tie, slipping on my black shoes, pulling up my socks, my garters. Petra was in early making me French toast, the greasy pan-hot smell levitating in the kitchen, adding to my dull queasy over tiredness, but I scoffed it down anyway, smearing a dollop of tomato sauce across its soggy sizzled surface. Behind me Dad hovered between the kitchen and passage, a vague transmitter of the armoured tension which wired out from my sister's room. There'd been no sign of any of them. He was too afraid, I think, to go in there, enter that hardened female space, disturb the disturbed, and I was too afraid to ask him how they were, to force an answer to an impossible question.

Dad wouldn't leave the women alone so Uncle Rob swung by to give me a lift. I snatched my satchel from my bedroom floor and fled, welcoming the chance to escape the house. We drove along listening to old Shania Twain songs blaring through the CD player. Uncle Rob tapped his fingers on the steering wheel, though when I looked closely I realised they were not in time to the music, but a half-beat out, and I found this odd, something I didn't connect to being a nervous tick, one sign of several to pass my thirteen year old brain those coming weeks.

He dropped me off at the gates of school, thumbing about to give me five bucks for some tuck at break. He patted my leg hesitantly, unartfully, as I jumped out the car, an action he had second thoughts about, perhaps realising that touching the leg of a boy my awkward age would cause offence, mistaken now as an act of intrusion.

I WENT IN THROUGH THE GATES, managing to dodge the sullen duty prefect and slipped into registration class where my mood changed instantly. I had a coup to muster attention with, a great story to tell. I had black and bruised wrists from banging at my bedroom door to accentuate the drama. I held them up, showing everyone, garnering gasps of jealous wonder. Everyone was more drawn to me than usual because I'd been through something. They wanted to know all the details, so I elaborated, drawing on the stock of my present currency. The additions went down a treat and I loved being the royal toast of my class.

It was all a big joke and only my English teacher, Mrs Ellis, put a stop to it in period three, telling me to buckle down, get on with our usual Monday morning essay about 'what we did on the weekend'. I scribbled away, taking even more licence, adding in a bit where a shot was fired and Dad tackled one of them to the floor, sending a glass cabinet with Mom's expensive china smashing to smithereens. For once my pen flowed easily, effortlessly. I handed my work in with a knowing inner smirk, triumphant certainty my take on the weekend's events was a shoe-in for a Special Commendation.

But Mrs Ellis didn't comment. She donned her glasses, read it silently, pensively, hardly awed by the story at all.

What was wrong with the bloody woman? She didn't make any attempt to mark my writing, to correct my normal grammatical errors, chastise my unruly spider scrawl handwriting, and when she reached the end all she said was, 'Alright Danny, sit down now.' She closed my book, pushed it to the edge of her desk.

AT BREAK I was playing soccer with the usual gang when I noticed the figure of Pastor Andrews standing on the side of our field, the usual cool wide white smile across his face, summoning me. I ran over to him.

'Young Walker,' he said. 'How are we mister?'

'I'm fine sir,' I said.

'I hear you've had a nasty incident over the weekend?'

'Yes sir.'

'Poor boy. These imbeciles, hey?'

'Yes sir.'

'What a terrible thing. How's your family coping?'

'We're fine sir.'

'And your sister, how is she?'

'She's okay sir.'

'Awful. Frightful.'

'Yes sir.'

'And how are you child? You feeling alright?'

'Yes sir, I'm fine.'

'Okay, well I'm sorry you've had to go through all this. You let me know if you want to talk about it, yes?'

'Yes sir.'

'Just be strong and supportive to your mom and dad and your sister, okay?'

'Yes sir.'

'Good boy, run along now.'

AFTER BREAK I was sitting in biology, dotty Miss Rothwell's droll voice wavering in and out of my ears, something dull about the habits of honey bees, when I began to feel queasy. Soon I was rushing to the bathroom, then kneeling over the toilet bowl vomiting. I was sweating, my brow drenched, my limbs going numb beneath me. I stood in front of the mirror splashing water onto my face. I looked white as paper, this pounding headache, a sharp stabbing pain behind my eyes. Then I was sick again.

One of the older boys found me slumped against the toilet cubicle, shaking and shivering. Looking up at him, lifting my heavy slouched head from my neck, was a struggle, but I saw him standing stock still over me, his mouth gaping, then he was gone. The san nurse rushed in, now I was on the move, being escorted to sick bay, frog-marched between Fruity and some other boy. The ground seemed muddy beneath me, a churning, depthless slime-pit. I was unsure of my footing, how or where to place each step.

I DON'T REMEMBER GETTING HOME, but I was there.

'It must've been something bad I ate,' I told Mom.

All I wanted in the whole world was to lie down and be comforted by my own cool snug bed, to sleep unwatched and unattended for a while, but Mom insisted Dad take me to the doctor straight away.

'I don't want to go,' I cried. 'It's just something I ate, I told you.'

'You must, Danny,' she insisted.

'Only if you take me.'

'I can't leave Becca, now just go with your father please.'

'I don't want to.'

'Danny! Stop being difficult, *please!*'

I went with Dad. We sat together, endlessly silent,

slumped in the cheerless cream-walled waiting room of our GP's practice. Eventually Dr Phillips called us in and gave me some fat sour-tasting pills to swallow with warm water from a small plastic cup and then, unannounced, a jab squat in the middle of my arm with a long needle. It stung like a bitch, I cried briefly, trying to complain, but at once I felt drowsy, surfacing in a strange fog when we were squealing to an abrupt stop and I was nearly being flung off the back seat of the Hilux. Dad was hammering his fists at the hooter, yelling, 'Useless fucking *munts*, learn to fucking drive.'

I WOKE UP FROM THE LONGEST SLEEP. It was the next day, I could sense the lightness of morning air, the slant summer sun slipping over my bedcovers. It was hot again. The rainclouds had slinked off, the bright blueness of the summer sky, now washed of its dusty rawhide hue, replacing them. I climbed out of bed and stumbled outside, not noticing if anyone had noticed me. My shoulders felt knotted, my jellied legs heavy. I threw myself, knees tucked up to my chest, into the pool. The shock-cold plunge rushed my body, I felt instantly light, levitating for a moment, suspended blithely. While I was down there a momentary glimmer floated up in my mind, a clear instantaneous remembrance of what had happened, followed by a condensed vision beyond boyhood into this liquid darkness, utterly frightening. I drew my arms up, kicking off the bottom of the pool, struggling through a swarming silver column of effervescence towards the surface.

A spray of water must have mushroomed up over me when I dive-bombed in, its flat explosive sound levelling outwards because when I re-emerged the dogs were yelping ecstatically, darting round the edges, and coming towards me was Mom, a long strident shape, stiff with intent.

126

'Danny, what the hell are you doing?' she shouted. 'You damn well nearly gave us all a heart attack.'

'What?' I said, stroking the water off my face, 'I'm just going for a swim.'

'Well your sister's trying to sleep.'

'Sorry,' I said, gripped with panic, 'Becca, is she okay?'

She looked down at me, relaxation pressing at her shoulders. 'Yes, Danny, just keep it down, okay my boy.'

'Yes Mom.'

Then she said, 'you alright Danny?'

'Yes,' I replied.

'You sure?'

'I'm sure.'

She turned back to the house. I clambered out and sat on the ledge of the pool, overworking my legs to churn furiously at the water. The roiling wake alerted the dogs again and they stood to attention, their ears erect, their wet muzzles lowered to the surface of the bubbling water. Just as one was about to yelp I squeezed her jaws shut tight with both hands, forcing her to cower.

'Shhh,' I whispered in her ears, 'we can't wake Becca.'

WHEN I LOOKED OUTWARDS from the pool I noticed some commotion at the far end of our yard, in the corner where the two walls met at right angles. There was a rolled truncation of wire dangling over the wall like the skeleton of a snake, bobbling, self-energised, scraping the top of the wall as it sprung back and forth. I looked at it for a while, intrigued as the wire rasped against the brickwork. The face of a black man popped up behind it, puppet-like, a gangly head on a stick. Another walked through the electric gate which was standing open. He was wearing those blue workman's overalls.

I was up, cantering my wet feet across the lawn, past the veranda, towards the back of the house. I scrambled in via the kitchen door, the dogs bounding at heel. Petra's square rump was anchored at the sink, she was scouring a pot with steel wire. Her flabby upper arms scrubbing away were an attractive comfort so I threw myself round her waist, burying my head in her damp, pink polka dot apron. Lemon-scented scum filled my nose.

'Mister Danny,' she said. 'What is the matter?'

I stood away from her, steadying up.

'Where's the boss?' I asked.

'What's wrong?'

'The boss, where is he?'

Aunty Jackie was standing in the doorway.

'What's the matter my boy? You look like you've seen a ghost.'

'There's some men,' I said, 'they're in our yard, the gate's open.'

'It's alright Danny. Just relax.'

'But they're in blue.'

'Blue what?'

'Blue overalls!'

'It's just some workers putting up a security fence for your dad, that's all, nothing to be worried about. Come, let me pour you some juice. You look as flushed as anything.'

I staggered to the middle of the kitchen, realising how laboured my breathing was. My chest was swelling with each intake, my lungs bloating against my ribcage. The sweat across my brow dripped down my cheeks. Aunt Jackie handed me a glass of cold litchi juice from the fridge. I took it but had to steady the glass to my lips with both trembling hands.

FROM THE LOUNGE WINDOWS I watched cautiously all morning as those two men, under Dad's beady eye, inched along the top of the wall, drilling, hammering, bending, bolting what I was told was a high-voltage electric fence, complete with coiled barbwire, interlooped with strips of razor cable.

I was not comfortable seeing them, despite telling myself I was being childish and irrational.

Mom was not pleased either.

'That whole damn contraption looks like a manic depressive's attempt at an art installation,' she said to Aunt Jackie, a rare occasion when they had both suspended their watch over my sister, coming into the lounge for late morning tea.

'It's for the best,' Aunt Jacks said, unknotting the muscles in her shoulders, stretching her neck. 'Give you all a bit of peace of mind, hey.'

Mom nodded, faintly tolerant, sipping her tea, looking out through the window. There were tears beginning to gleam in her glazed, tired eyes.

I CREPT TOWARDS MY SISTER'S ROOM, slowly sliding myself through the opening of the half shut door, petrified it may creak, even mutedly on its hinges. I feared that unheard sound, that it's rendering would signify my illicit presence, finally trigger the slow dissolving drip of my crystallized guilt. I held myself together with a deep breath, standing just inside the room, looking on through the murky orange light. A tall standing fan with a large visor-like face billowed out a motorised flow of harried air, rotating on its axis regimentally, a sentinel posted guard. I was relieved for this ticking purr, breaking the awful burden of silence I'd been anticipating. It allowed me to stand undetected in its murmur, calibrate my feelings, a still figure in the peripheral dark of my sister's grief. All I could make out was a heaped shape under the bedcovers, the small likeness of mass, the round sloping contours of the back of a head, a flattened, fevered shag of hair, but I couldn't gather any information, any certainty of movement, consciousness of any kind. I couldn't see her eyes in that light. They were most likely turned away from me anyhow, cast unseeing towards a dull splurge of wall. I couldn't tell whether she was looking at me while I was looking at her.

NEXT THEY WERE RUNNING rampant in the house. A different team of men, four this time, arriving in a small white Nissan Bantam truck, wearing smart beige trousers, black belts, tucked-in green golf shirts with a logo on the left breast pocket. A short, stocky white guy with a smeary bald head, a sharp black goatee, took charge. He was chatting to Dad as they watched the men, squashed into corners of the ceilings, contorted up fancy aluminium ladders which folded down in a series of neat metallic clicks each time they were moved.

'Yeah, these bloody *tsotsis*,' he said, 'like a blinking plague.'

The flash of a tight grimace across Dad's sober face signalled his agreement. He was watching with fanatical concentration. This steely resolve in his eyes as he stood there patiently, taking everything in, looking at the ceilings, down along walls, his mind calculating to ensure every area of the house would now be watched by this robotic guard dog we were bringing to live with us, a fierce infrared hound.

In the space of an afternoon our house was wired-up with a minefield of security gadgets. Door-stop alarms to be wedged under every door at night, a centralised internal alarm system so advanced it dialled a designated cell phone when it detected an intruder. LED cameras wired up to stream images on a rotating cycle to a computer monitor fixed to the floor below Dad's side of the bed. They rigged up state of the art panels with laser sensors, front-surface mirrors, optical receivers with audible buzzers that bleated every time anything came near them on the outside walls. Dad and I were walked through the whole complex process as everything was checked, passwords set which Dad claimed only we would ever know. Sharp bleeps and alarms flared round the house in short spurts as tests were done and at the end the stocky man declared that our house now resembled a permanent convention centre for the security industry.

'Chum,' he said, 'nothing is getting in this place and that I can guarantee.'

'Well, we'll see,' Dad said.

'Honestly I've never done such an advanced or intricate set-up as this. I'd almost say you've gone overboard, but, look, I appreciate your position and all. Trust me, the bastards won't get within twenty-five metres of the place.'

'That had better be right,' Dad said.

THAT NIGHT WE WERE SUBJECTED to the unrelenting machinations of a crazed mechanical monster. Ear-piercing sirens screeched out with random intermittence, just when we were on the verge of at last nodding off. Dad lumbered off the bed next to me, went ranging around the house, beeping reset buttons, making mistakes, trying again, his patience tested by the sharp staccato bleats which indicated some error. He fell gruffly back to bed. Then those over-zealous external sensors activated, probably a large spider, a rat or lizard, and a loud high-frequency buzzing blared out from a horn wired up over the fridge. Dad lurched and stumbled, torch and crowbar in hand, out towards the yard in a mad, sedentary panic. Back again, he fumbled in the dark at the control pad, pressing more buttons. He lay down, this soldierly stiffness shrunk right through him, pressing inwards, towards the hard centre of his knotted nerves. I pretended to be asleep. I sat up sometime in the early hours of the morning, an automated reaction to the stale heat, this savage tension sprung through the room. I looked across to see Dad lying on his side, his sad eyes wide, marble black in the dark, unblinking, transfixed by those scrolling monochrome interiors flickering on a screen.

I SUSPECT DAD HAD BARELY SLEPT a second since the attack and early the following morning when I was up eating the breakfast that Petra had slapped together, there was a moment when he forgot one of the dog's names. He was standing in the kitchen, his shoulders bent, his hair wild, an unshaven grey mat rolled across his gaunt cheeks, sharp stubble on his chin, and he was muttering senselessly as our little Jack Russell leapt around his feet, yelping and barking. Mom came, slipping in unseen from the passage, and forced three small white pills down his throat while she led him underarm back to the bedroom, whispering smooth, soothing sayings in his ears.

PASTOR ANDREWS CORNERED ME by the music block as I was coming round the side of the main auditorium where we'd been having our weekly class thrash around on a set of marimbas.

'Oh Daniel, I've been meaning to come and find you my friend, but you didn't seem to be around yesterday?

'No sir,' I said, 'I was absent.'

'Oh, everything alright?'

'Yes sir.'

'I mean I know everything's really far from alright, but are you all coping?'

'Yes sir.'

'And your family, how are they?'

'We're all fine sir.'

'You sure?'

'Yes sir, sure.'

'I'm here if you want to come and chat. Don't be shy.'

'Yes sir, thank you.'

DAD WAS WORKING HIMSELF into an all-consuming frenzy and the great fortification of the Walker house was a mania I suspected my family would never escape. Now the large shrub by the gate had been hacked down, the leopard tree by the wall sawn into pieces, any bush or plant thicker than a pencil shaft consigned to the compost heap. He'd done this himself. He was in the driveway as Uncle Rob swept in with me, bare-chested, barefooted in boxer shorts, his feet and legs grimed with dirt, an oiled film of sweat lacquered over his torso. He was hobbled down pushing the wheelbarrow piled high with his branchy cull.

'Hey, garden boy,' Uncle Rob said, standing in the drive, clicking his fingers at Dad, 'come wash my car. Then, while you're at it, polish my shoes.'

Dad gave him a wry smile. 'Piss off white man,' he said.

He walked us over all he'd done, telling us his theory.

'Those bastards hid in the shrub by the gate,' he said, pointing to the absent mound of space by the intercom. 'They were there, behind it, just waiting for one of us to come in or go out. It was that flipping easy for them. Can you believe how lax we've been all this time?'

Uncle Rob and I looked down at the bare patch of earth, remnants of roots. I remembered the ginger-striped cat scurrying from the shrub, scaling the wall, flushed from its dense nest. I recalled that trio of men trailing me up the hill, then ranging down behind me. I imagined them there, outside our yard, pressing the intercom, seeking me out, this arrogant little shit of a white kid, wanting to put me in my place. Maybe if I'd had the balls to climb out the pool, the guts to stand there at the gate while they told me off, take the bollocking I was due, they wouldn't have come back a few nights later.

'YOU DON'T THINK they could have just scaled the wall any time they bloody well wanted to?' Uncle Rob said. 'I mean, let's face it, it wasn't the most formidable of walls to start with.'

'No, no,' Dad replied. 'All these damn bushes and hedges. We've been so bloody stupid all this time. Just giving them the perfect fucking opportunity.'

'Maybe,' Uncle Rob said.

'You give these *munts* an inch and they take a bloody mile. No. They've been biding their time while we've been far too trusting and carefree. I tell you we've been lulled into a false sense of security all these years, literally. What were we bloody thinking? If it wasn't this lot, then it would have been another bunch. Sooner or later. Mark my words.'

DAD CRACKED OPEN TWO BEERS. Uncle Rob and he sat out on the veranda. It was lunchtime, it was hot. I was paddling round in the pool, degreasing my skin from the sticky layered sweat stacked over me from an aimless school day. Aunt Jackie came out, joined the men. She was combing out her long auburn hair, newly wet from the shower. She slid down onto Uncle Rob's lap and he kissed her on the cheek, running his hand playfully along her thigh.

'How's she doing?' he asked quietly.

She made a gesture with her right hand, her non-committal way of saying, so-so. Not great, not good. Just so-so.

Aunty Jackie looked tired, despite just taking a shower, a tight, haggard look weighing on her entire body.

'You poor girls,' Uncle Rob said, giving her another kiss on the neck. She laid her head on his chest.

Wading in the deep end, sucking the pool water in, then jetting it out in a pattering fountain, I watched all this unfold with quiet attention, eavesdropping in plain sight. I was looking for clues about my sister, compelled to learn the nuances of this adult alphabet of gestures. I caught Dad's eyes and noticed him staring at me observing my aunt and uncle in this telling moment. He could tell I was becoming attuned to the languages of the skin and the body, the truth spoken behind mundane talk, revealed between the clipped, strangled silences.

'Any more luck getting any info out of JVS?' Uncle Rob asked.

'Nah,' Dad said, 'bloody hoods. Who am I kidding? You won't get them to admit to anything anyway. These *munt* owned banks. Nothing but elaborate vaults to stash the loot from government scams. They all cover for their own. One big bloody testament to corruption. That was one colossal fricking trap I should've seen coming if ever there was one!'

'Jesus Christ, you have to love this country,' Uncle Rob stated. 'Only in fecking Africa!'

Hearing Dad's words while treading the close-bound wrap of water somehow rekindled the feeling of being inside that ever enfolding labyrinth of passages and rooms in James's mansion. The notion I was somehow being led all that way to his room for a purpose, his own design to trap me in all that wealth, the political sanctuary of his father's ironclad connections. Perhaps our testy exchange of words had been laced with even more malice than I'd supposed, the result of pitting two jealous boys together, one white, one black, both our father's true sons, while above and beyond all that masonry and glass and tiling, Dad too was being baited into a kind of devastating trap. I couldn't quite shake this separate, distant feeling of uneasy guilt about that night, something I now realised simmered more urgently with my father.

When Uncle Rob left, Aunt Jackie went with him, her travel bag dropped on the back seat of their white Nissan Navara. She and Mom stood in the driveway hugging, rocking gently together, holding each another for a long time.

'Thanks so much, Jacks,' Mom said, squeezing her closer.

'I'm so sorry you've had to go through this.'

'You've been amazing,' Mom said.

'I'm just five minutes up the road, so I'll be back in a flash to help out. Just pick up the phone.' Aunt Jackie hugged me next. 'Be strong for everyone my Danny boy.'

'Thanks Aunt Jacks,' I said, 'I will be.'

AROUND FOUR O'CLOCK a short, professional looking woman with thin stringy ginger hair arrived in a small chrome coloured Toyota Corolla hatchback. She was dressed in a mauve suit with a white blouse, a pendant attached to her left lapel. There were letters inscribed on it, an emblem, she was either a nurse or a counsellor. She had come on an official visit. Oh God, I thought, that's all I need. She sat forward on the edge of the couch, her posture very erect. There was a practised air about her, used to coming into the homes of people like us, battered, shell-shocked, in distress.

She smiled at me and said, 'Hello mister.'

'Danny,' Mom said, 'why not go and play nicely with the dogs outside, hey my love.'

This was my cue to leave the adults to their grown-up talk. I padded round the garden for a bit, throwing a bald slobbered tennis ball the length of the wall for the dogs to race. The wall was stark now, the brown patches against the dull white-washed slabs like a set of imprinted prehistoric footprints, the rutted gouges of fine red soil where Dad had hacked out the shrubs and hedges were plain ugly. To make it worse, leaning over us, a rolled tunnel of barbwire. If that ginger stray were to scale the wall now, I imagined she would gut herself.

There was no one in the lounge now. I noticed the door to Becca's room shut, muffled voices purring behind it, that lady's, firm and distinctive, then, after a pause, the brittle replies of my sister, sometimes prompted by Mom or Dad. I listened, my ears as close to the door as I could level them. The shape of words defied me, barrelled and hushed, I struggled to decipher their vague meaning, measure their grave seriousness in relation to every screechy stretch of silence. The longer they hung, the more excruciating. I couldn't make anything out. The exclusion was killing, closeted out there, absorbing the transmission of my sister's horror, sponging up my parent's suffering.

My stomach felt loose all of a sudden. I spun round, dashing to the bathroom, pulling my pants down, squatting on the toilet seat just in time as my bowels began to run.

TO ADD TO EVERYTHING ELSE NEW about the house, Dad bought a revolver. It was long-barrelled, slender, silver A. Smith & Weston 686.38 Special. He said he'd spent the day going through this complicated process to license it, in the end paying a backhander to the cops to have it fast-tracked. It sat on the armrest of his chair, inches away, slid a third of the way into its beige beaten leather holster, balanced and ready. Despite my affiliations to plastic guns, my proficiency with an automatic machine gun on video games, I didn't like this real version one bit. Mom could tell I was on edge about it. She took me aside to the kitchen.

'There's a sacrifice we have to make from now on, Danny,' she said, 'and that gun is it, okay? It means we can carry on.'

'Okay Mom.'

'You sure you understand?'

'Yes,' I said.

THAT NIGHT I WAS ALLOWED the small mercy of sleeping in my own room. I stirred in the early hours from a bad dream, Dad ranging about with a *badza*, hacking at those shrubs, trees, hedges. The blade wheeling and whipping, plumes of dust, chunks of hurtling vegetation. I woke, sweat across my brow, lying curled up on my side thinking of those men sauntering down the hill. I saw their eyes, we connected. Something uneasy passed between us.

I heard Mom's footsteps so I stumbled into the passage. The light was horridly bright, heightening my grogginess, but I could see the outline of her figure. She was wearing a white nightdress, I believed she was coming to comfort me. I'd maybe called out for her in my dream, seeking her warm Nivea waxed hands in the longing clasp of mine. But her back was to me, standing in Rebecca's doorway.

'Mom,' I whispered.

She turned to me, her face ghostly white.

'Just go back to bed Danny,' she said.

AT SCHOOL MY MATES WERE TALKING about the end of term dance. When I got home I went to see if there were signs of Amy next door. I'd only replied very briefly to the messages she'd sent asking if we were all okay. Halfway across the lawn it occurred to me that our little arrangement had been thwarted. I'd never be able to hop over the wall again, our occasional rendezvous, trysts behind the rockery, were gone. Closer to the coffee shade tree I saw that many of its overhanging branches had been savagely hacked back, most of it was now a ragged stump. I levered myself up between it and the wall, poking my head over. But with this rolling mass of thick steel wire, barbed, bladed with razor-sharp edges, plus the thought that my nose was just a couple of inches away from an almighty electric zap, the view now just didn't seem the same.

I REMINDED MOM.

'Of course we haven't forgotten, my boy,' she said. 'We'd better go and get you kitted out.'

She was tired and I felt guilty, but she left Dad in charge of Becca and we set off for Sam Levy's Village. We browsed in Edgars, then went to Truworths Man where I tried on a smart black striped suit, picked out a red shirt, a jazzy tie.

'You can wear your school shoes with this can't you?'

'No Mom,' I said, 'but I'll wear my black sneakers. That'll look cool.'

'Okay,' she said.

She took me to Chita's for a strawberry milkshake, waffles with syrup and hazelnut ice cream. We sat by a

139

table next to some wide bright green palm fronds, Mom looking at me as I sucked on the straw of my sickly sweet shake. She leaned over, brushing the hair off my forehead.

'Danny, I'm sorry I've been so preoccupied with Becca and everything,' she said, 'I know I've been neglecting you something horrid.'

'Don't worry Mom, it's fine.'

She was smiling at me, but looked sad as well, something very tight drawing the skin of her face closer to the bones, a rigid mask.

'You okay Danny?'

'Yes.'

'Are you sure? You've been such a good boy.'

'Yes I'm fine mom,' I said. 'Are you okay?'

'Yes I'm doing okay.'

'Are you sure? And Becca?' I asked, 'how's she?'

The tightness on her face pulled slightly at the sides as she swallowed a sip of my milkshake.

'She'll be fine.'

TOWARDS DUSK a select group of Rebecca's friends arrived in a blue VW GOLF GTI. They walked up the drive in solemn procession, quietly tip-toeing into the house as if treading on eggshells. They brought flowers, chocolates, gift bags. They whispered when they came into the hallway, hugging Mom and Dad, saying how sorry they were, the tears beginning to flow again, never a dry eye in the house. I hated to see my mother so upset, every new tear was becoming a drag on me.

They proceeded into Becca's room, the door closing after them. They stayed for hours, not a sound emerging. I walked past, skulking up and down the passage. No one came in or went out. They just seemed to migrate there,

140

into this strange dark interior, with the curtains drawn, the light dull, a formless weight in the centre of the bed which must have been my sister, though I'd seldom caught a glimpse of her those last five days.

Then they all trailed off, teary eyed as they came. Mom took Becca's dinner to her on a tray but I noticed it came out barely touched. I stood in the kitchen by the scullery. Petra was washing up dishes.

'What are you doing Mister Danny?' she said.

'Nothing,' I replied.

I realised I'd done this three or four times now, forming the habit of inspecting Becca's leavings, this food picked at on a plate the only evidence I saw of my sister nowadays.

DAD WAS ON THE PHONE to Travis Bell, pressing him to chop down the thick hedge by his wall, across the road. From what was being said, the rising flat tone of Dad's voice, Travis wasn't playing ball.

'But maybe his stubbornness is a good thing,' Mom said to me in the kitchen. 'I mean where does it all stop? It's the Bells' hedge, then the Riverstones', then the Moyos', then the Stavrous' and before you know it the whole road is a bare ugly monument to paranoia. Then they'll have won, won't they?'

'I guess,' I said.

I tended to agree with my father. We couldn't afford to give those motherfuckers even the sniff of another opportunity.

LATER ON A MIRACLE. Becca surfaced from her dark hibernation, emerging from her room. Mom and Dad walked on either side of her, supporting her under arm, helping her, encouraging her along with each small step.

141

I was standing in the dining room looking through the lounge when I saw her being led along, dead slow, as if in some out-dated ritual. Her arms were held out as though she'd lost her sense of balance, her feet unsteadily falling one in front of the other. It wasn't my sister shuffling about, just an outer frame. She wore a creased pale blue nightie, her hair flattened against the back of her scalp, framing the sides of her scarlet pillow-bruised face. She lay on the couch, staring absently at the TV.

I didn't know what to do, or say. I stood dead still, desperately wanting her to be stood up again, walked back to her room, slid back into her bed, covered up with her duvet. I'd longed to see her all this time, and now I was a faltering mess. I saw Mom gesturing to me, mouthing at me to open my dry mouth, move my leaden heavy tongue, say something nice to my ailing sister.

'Hi Becca,' I managed to mutter, taking a step into the lounge.

'Hi Danny,' she whispered, 'sorry, I didn't see you there.'

Mom and Dad were fidgety and attentive around her. Mom sat beside her combing out her hair with long drawn strokes. It looked painful, but Becca didn't show the slightest expression of discomfort. Dad fetched a big bowl of crisps, poured Becca a glass of fresh fruit juice he placed on a side table, within easy reach. The whole time she didn't touch the juice or the crisps. I sat stiffly on the far side of the couch pretending, like everyone else, I was watching *QI*. I shot quick sideways glances at her, each time hoping I'd catch a glimpse of the pretty, fun-loving Becca of old, that some faint glimmer of her would fight through to liven the deadpan expression on that plastic face, brighten those cold glassed eyes. There was nothing. Her stillness was impenetrable, bouncing any advances off in waves, riddling me with fright. My hands were shaking, my jaw chattering.

I WOKE UP LATER IN THE NIGHT feeling queasy. I rushed to the toilet, my stomach cramping, then loosening. Leaving the bathroom I took a step too far to the right setting off one of the alarms. The siren blared out all over, arresting me, frozen under the stark shower of the light bulb in the passage. Dad was up at once, stalking with a truncheon, all hell breaking out about the house.

DURING REGISTRATION we were told to go to the hall where Pastor Andrews and the Headmaster, Mr Jameson, gave us lectures about how to behave at the dance the following night. Pastor Andrews told us about this thing called etiquette, how to be well mannered round the girls. We all thought it was a hoot and when someone caught a case of the giggles halfway into his bit about how best to compliment a girl on her nice dress, it spread to all of us, soon one large raucous chorus, hosing with laughter.

'Alright damn it, that's enough,' said Mr Jameson, but he was grinning to himself as well. 'Let's just end it there by saying that you had better all be on your very best behaviour, right? No funny business from any of you little sods.'

Afterwards everyone was chattering about the big night so I decided now was the time to boast about having secured my prize date, the hot, desirable Amy Whitaker.

'No ways,' said Fruity.

'I'm not kidding,' I said.

'Jesus you're lucky,' another of my mates said, 'I know someone who went out with Amy Whitaker, a cousin of mine. She's well fit and she lets you squeeze her tits if you ask her nicely.'

'Hey, that can't be true,' I said, but everyone by now was chanting, 'Ha ha, Walker's gonna get some action, Walker's gonna get some action,' slapping me on the back, high-fiving me.

'You've got to do it,' Fruity said to me later, just before we went into our maths class, 'at least promise me you'll try.'

'Of course I'll try,' I said, 'why wouldn't I?'

'You're going to be so lucky Walks.'

This banter put me into a cheery mood and at break, for the first time since that Monday, I felt spirited enough to make my usual concerted effort in our daily soccer match. I charged about the field, buoyed with all kinds of new possibilities filling my head, the chanting envy of my friends still buzzing through me.

THAT EVENING MOM AND DAD ushered Becca out into the lounge again. It was early on, Mom tending to dinner, so Dad was left to dote on her. Now that I saw them together I noticed how stiff he'd become in her presence, just as much at a loss as me.

They'd always been so close. I remember when we were very young Becca was forever clinging round Dad's neck, or reclining on his lap. He would sit kneading her hair as she dozed. Framed pictures in the house show him giving her piggyback rides on the beach in Durban, both beaming broadly into the camera, bleached wind-stung sand on their faces, another of them holding hands walking a wet woodland trail of pines in the mountains.

But now he was afraid to touch her, fearing she may fracture. He hovered round her nervously, outside her bedroom door, never quite going in, orbiting her sphere like I did, or tonight eagerly puffing up the cushions on

144

the couch before she flopped down, curling herself into a ball.

I made a point of greeting her with exaggerated care, careful to ask if she wanted anything. I offered to make her tea, bring her cake or crisps. She responded with indifference, sometimes managing a weak smile, other times mumbling a series of half-formed grunts. She looked tired, her eyes drooping and dull. Sitting on the couch she was forever dropping off to sleep.

After a while Dad went out with the dogs, torch and truncheon in hand. Alone with her at last, I emboldened myself, deciding I was the one who had to break this icy stalemate.

'Beccs,' I said, 'are you okay?'

There was a pause before she answered, then she said, 'I'm fine Danny.'

Her voice was brittle, hollow, weak. She looked up at me, her eyes hard set on mine. She'd said three plain words to me but it was somehow an entire conversation, fraught, uneasy. She had tears in her eyes. When Dad came back in and saw, she began to sob the second he mentioned it.

'Daniel, what the hell have you done to upset her?'

'Nothing,' I said, 'I just asked her how she is, that's all.'

'For Christ sake, you know she's not well so why go making it worse by asking?'

'I'm sorry.'

I couldn't win. Whatever I said would have been wrong. When Dad's punishing glare shifted from me to Becca, I quietly slipped from the room, hiding out of sight for the rest of the evening in my bedroom.

WITH THE LIGHTS OUT I tried to think about positive things. I thought back to talk of Amy and wondered how soft and supple her breasts might feel pushed into the cupped palm of my hand, whether I might be able to trace the outline of her nipples, what that glorious possibility might feel like. We might kiss again, my lips pressed ever so briefly against the moist pinkness of hers, our wet tongues momentarily touching. My hand slipped into my briefs, I was fondling myself, but nothing seemed to be stirring. I remained soft and limp. These randy imaginings weren't right anyway, not with all that had been happening, the chastened atmosphere misting through our house. I turned on my side, clenching my stomach, moaning in the dark as I felt the cramps ease into place, ready to grip me, knowing any second I'd have to lurch off my bed, make a dash for the bathroom.

IT WAS TRADITIONAL FOR PARENTS to attend the Headmaster's cocktail hour before the dance started, so arrangements were made for Becca to go to Aunt Jackie and Uncle Rob's for the night.

At half-five we were ready. Dad was in a suit, Mom looking elegant in a pearl-coloured dress. I raided Dad's toiletry shelf, drenched myself in his Old Spice cologne, its manly fragrance stirring my mood. I was in the bathroom styling my hair when I heard Mom talking to Becca.

'My girl, you'll be okay,' she was saying, 'we'll only be gone for a couple of hours, see, then we can come and fetch you from Rob's and Jackie's if you'd prefer.'

I didn't hear what Becca was on about, but after a few minutes Mom walked past towards her bedroom. I came into the passage to listen.

'She's not doing so well tonight, Dave,' she said.

'What's she saying?'

'She's having flashbacks again.'

'Bad ones?'

'It is Friday night after all. It's been exactly a week.'

'Should we get her to take a pill? Might calm her down a bit.'

'I don't know. I'd rather not. I'm just not comfortable coming to rely too much on pills and things. They're hell of a strong. If we're not careful, we'll have a whole other problem on our hands.'

'Let's ask Jacks and Rob to come here.'

'No, she won't hear of it. You know how she gets. Dave, I think I'd better stay.'

'No, no, you can't stay here alone, no ways. Bring her to the school with us.'

'In that state?'

'Well I'm not having you two stay here alone, it's out of the question.'

I'd heard enough. I dropped all caution to come storming into the doorway of Becca's room. A whole week had gone by, I wanted to tell her, we were all tired of it now, enough was enough. Yet despite the bright sunshine outside the curtains remained drawn, backlit with that same dusky, syrupy orange. It was so dull, how hadn't it driven her completely crazy by now? She was hugging a big continental pillow with a frilly cover, her long hair mattered across her face. She slowly cupped a hand over her ear, as if she anticipated my censure, blocking all notion of my existence. The sight disarmed me, this limp figment hankered down in a sad, stuffy enclosure, so I retreated.

I went back to my room, sat on the end of my bed. I had been on a high the whole day but in an instant felt deflated. All I could smell was the stupidity of my skin busy stewing in heady Old Spice, but inside me, the anticipation and excitement, drained away too. Sitting there I thought I might look exactly like Becca if she was standing in my doorway looking at me.

'Danny,' Dad said, 'look your sister isn't well, hey. So we're going to have to ask Tony and Monica to drive you and Amy to the dance. I'm sorry my boy, but it's just one of those things okay.'

'Yeah, okay Dad,' I said.

Mom escorted me next door. When the Whitaker's gate rolled back and I saw Amy come out into the driveway, looking lovely in her red dress, tears filled my eyes. I barely managed to slip the corsage Mom had given me onto her silky white wrist before breaking down. She looked so nice, we had made such an effort, and this was supposed to be my big night, the end of my dreaded first year of high school, but instead I was inconsolable, a petulant crying two year old.

'Oh there, there,' Monica said, 'Danny what's wrong my boy?'

'I think he's overwhelmed,' I heard Mom whisper. 'It's been a rollercoaster week. He's just upset.'

'Ah shame, Danny, there, there.'

Monica took my head in her hands, drawing me to her chest. She patted me on the shoulder as I sobbed against her. She was warm and comforting, but I was pining for the bliss of my own mother's touch against me, feeling her looming there, knowing there was nothing to equal it.

'I just hate this,' I blurted. 'I hate it so much!'

'I know Danny, there my boy, it's been a tough time for you guys hey. You're just upset, it'll be okay.'

We went to the dance. Amy was very nice about it. She held my hand in the back of the car, then at the dance too, making a point of smiling at me, so sweetly and innocently, whenever I found the nerve to look at her.

148

SATURDAY MORNING. Bright sunshine filtered to my feet and calves, rousing me from the first fulsome sleep I'd had in a week. Skittish memories from the dance flittered across my mind, framed by a balloon-encrusted ceiling wavering above everything, stark white, dark blue, suspended in this swollen firmament of dimpled clouds. We were determined to see every one exploded. Slung-shot gravel stones volleyed in secret from neckless ties, and somehow we got away with it, a spattering succession of bangs. The girls giggled at us with their sugary smiles. There were punch bowls with bloated floating fruit we drank from orange plastic cups. Oily samosas greased paper plates, chopped pink-skin frankfurters, mountains of crisps, rubbery Marshmallows. The comfort of a moist palm, Amy's bubbly sweetness, and all the while, at odds with everything, this overbidding numbness sunk right through me.

I STAGGERED TO THE LOUNGE and into a full-scale disagreement.

'Just take the bloody knife Jen,' Dad was saying, 'and leave it in the car, in the door, that's all I'm asking, just in case.'

'For the hundredth time, I'm *not* having that bloody thing anywhere near me,' Mom said.

'It's for your own good, damn it.'

'And what if it ends up in the blinking attacker's hands and not mine? Then what? I'm not up to fighting off a knife-wielding lunatic all by myself am I?'

Dad looked like a stark, gaunt study in tensed desperation.

'All I'm trying to do,' he yelled, 'is protect this bloody family, for Christ's sake!'

'Look, Dave, I've agreed to the pepper spray and a base-ball bat, and that's it, okay!'

He marched off, right past me. A door slammed and I swivelled back to glimpse Mom hurrying through the dining room, sniffling. I fled back to my room, slumped to the floor, electrically awake now. I very seldom heard my parents fight and never that tone in my father's voice. It sounded hollow, void, as if all his energy had discharged, washed out, leaving this flat automated redundancy.

I was sorry for my poor father. All this had disturbed him in a profound way. He was on edge now, always nervous, waiting for something out of the ordinary to occur. Though it wasn't his fault, the incident drew a line in his soul. After the ordeal it seemed he'd been fired through a crucible, every soft outer sentiment burned, stripped away, and what emerged was hard, iron cast. He blamed himself for what could never have been prevented.

LATER THAT MORNING they arrived, yet another work gang, welding, drilling, hammering, fixing up these big iron-gridded burglar bars that Dad ordered put up over every outside door, every window, every opening. The veranda was gridded in with thick black iron bars which looked no better, or were no less imprisoning when Mom immediately set me the task of painting them in gloss white. She feared that our long, wide veranda, where we often sat during those summer evenings, would now fall to disuse. The thought that the easy wicker chairs and garden set with a wrought iron table would just stand there, that the *braai* would quickly web over, the bodies of dead insects falling there, stiffening with time, was dismaying. That veranda opened up to the lush green grass, the crisp blue pool, but now those burglar bars were in, we knew we'd hardly ever sit there again.

Dad and I spent the afternoon rigging up a set of these high-powered spot lights all over the garden. He bought them at Lighting World. That night he flicked them on, I noted how sharp their glare was, intrusive, casting everything in a stark wash of sodium light. In bed I lay feeling sick in the fold of the brightness illuminating my curtains, holding me and the house in this stark, inquisitive tension, as if asking sensitive questions in some sort of sleazy reality show, the theatre spotlight trained on me until I answered, everyone waiting with baited breath, still figures in the electric dark.

THE NEXT DAY I asked Dad whether anything had become of the police investigation into our robbery.

'No,' he snapped, 'and don't hold your bloody horses over it either.'

'They must've found something out by now. They're the police!' I said.

'My boy, the sooner you realise that you're on your own in this bloody place the better, okay. No one's gonna lift a finger to help you unless there's a buck in it for themselves. Not the police, not this bloody corrupt government of ours, no one. It's the bloody mentality of this place, get used to it.'

'But that other cop who was here that night, the guy from Special Branch?'

'Dan, what have I just told you? They're bloody useless. Every one of them. They couldn't organise a piss up in a bloody brewery if you paid them.'

In just a week the rest of my family had lost their keenness for justice. It didn't seem a priority, it was absurd, as if what was done lost its consequences over time. They failed to believe anyone could ever be held accountable, or that we should attempt to retrieve the stolen money, Mom's jewellery. Instead they resigned to accepting there was this big gaping hole where what is valuable just vanishes, never seeing the light of day again.

I was the opposite. It was all black and white to me, a child's strong sense of right and wrong, the principle of paying for a criminal action non-negotiable. Justice was permanent, never losing relevance. If our case was solved, those thugs caught, everything would be fine again at home, our perfect former life restored. Then we needn't be so on edge the whole time, living in a caged box forever fearful. Over time we'd relax, our confidence returning. It was logical to assume those men must be somewhere, existing as physical beings, just in some unspecified location.

I SLIPPED FROM THE HOUSE as everyone had their Sunday afternoon rest, riding the ridge of Alice Smith, freewheeling down to the crescent ledge where the bottle store was. I skirted the periphery, peering in to that shabby interior as I glided by, expecting to find the shapes of those men, two tall, one stocky, lurking about, plotting, on the lookout for an opportunity. But I didn't see anything and never had the nerve to park my bike, skulk past the entrance for a closer look. Still, finding them was just a matter of calculation and perseverance.

ON MONDAY MORNING when walking up the slipway towards the entrance gates at school, I saw that Matt Chambers was the prefect on duty for the week. I hadn't given him a second thought since the robbery, we hadn't seen anything of him, but now his absence mounted up very quickly, a concrete slight against us, a grave insult towards my sister. What was his problem? I was uneasy seeing him, so I slipped into a stream of boys, hoping to be lost amongst them, and though holding my head down while walking through the gates, I noticed he had turned away.

AT HOME I TOOK A CHANCE phoning up that policeman from Special Branch. Dad had scribbled down his name and number in the phone book. It said, 'Police contact – SB – Zach, 0772835771.' The first two tries his number just rang. He was on another case, something important? Eventually he picked up.

'Mr Zach,' I began, 'I'm sorry to worry you.'

'Who is speaking?'

'I'm just phoning to ask if there is any update on a case you were investigating, a robbery at my house?'

He was silent for a moment.

'You say there was a disturbance?"

'Yes, an attack.'

'What house is that?'

'No. 11 Alice Smith Road. The Walker house.'

'Hold,' he said. 'No, there is nothing new to report.'

'You don't have any idea at all who was responsible? There were three men.'

'No, we have not apprehended any suspects to date. I'm sorry. It's unfortunate.'

I was about to hang up, but asked, 'do you think they could've belonged to a gang?'

'What is that?'

'I said, do you think it is possible they could have belonged to a gang, you know, that they go around doing that all the time?'

'It is possible.'

'Have there been any other attacks around our neighbourhood. I mean, do you think they might be related?'

'You may be right. It is possible. It may have been a gang

working that area. There might have been similar incidents at some other premises around that time, but there are no substantial leads. We are working on it.'

It was not much, but at least it was a small development. What other homes had been attacked? We hadn't heard of any, normally such news spread fast. But we lived in an extensive neighbourhood, Zach's reference to the area could have meant anything. When I phoned him a second time he was abrupt, ill-tempered. I was just a boy, he complained, my father should be making the inquiries, I was wasting police time.

I FORMULATED THIS IDEA. I would play the star detective, find out which other homes had been attacked, put the pieces of the puzzle together. Then I'd hand over the information, doing my bit to speed up the case. I harboured the fantasy one day soon we would catch up with those three *tsotsis*. I imagined what I'd do to them if we ever apprehend them. If Inspector Zach phoned me up one day and said, 'Mr Daniel Walker, we've got those three suspects, we have arrested them. They are here, in our cells. Come down and see for yourself. Come and sort them out if you want to. They are all yours. We cannot be bothered with them, but someone has to do it.'

THE NEXT DAY it wasn't so easy avoiding Matt Chambers. I was dropped off earlier than usual, very few groups of students I could hide amongst. If I hung back waiting for one to form, I'd only look conspicuous, so I quickened my step, striding towards the gates as if there was nothing the matter.

'Morning Sir,' I said, barely looking at him.

'Walker,' he replied, the slightest of nods.

I breezed on but was angered by his attitude. Something about the way my body might have tensed, or my expression hardened, alerted him because when I briefly glanced back, he had turned to face me and was staring at me with this blank, fixed expression. Arsehole, I thought. I couldn't help shake my head slightly as I moved forward, a dismissive gesture I knew was also meant to provoke him.

MY FIRST FREE AFTERNOON I set out on my bike with the intention of trying to quiz the maids and gardeners about the neighbourhood. I couldn't find out much myself, no one took me seriously. I sent Petra to go see what she could find out on the bush telegraph. Before long before she was back.

'Mr Danny,' she said, 'No. 5 Clairewood and No. 24 Kirby. They both have *tsotsis* come with guns, just like here.'

'Well done,' I said.

I rode to 24 Kirby first. It was a large property with an immaculately mown pavement, a straight row of five wide-trunked palm trees, their lime green foliage fanning out elegantly. Its wall was high red brick, a black electric gate. I had no idea who lived here but pressed the intercom and waited. The voice of a man answered.

'Hi, if it's okay, could I have a word with you about something please?' I asked.

'About what?'

'I'm just asking a few questions about some burglaries that have happened around here.'

'Burglaries? Okay, hold on.'

Footsteps came crunching down the shale driveway. The gate opened, a well-set middle aged man appearing.

'Hi, I'm Daniel Walker. I live at 11 Alice Smith.'

'Yes.'

'Well the Friday before last we had an attack at our house. Three men held us up with guns and stole money and my mom's jewellery from our safe. I was just wondering, I mean now that makes three attacks that we know of, and I thought maybe there are similarities between what happened to us and what happened here.'

'Here? Are you sure?'

'I think so.'

'Who told you there'd been a break in here?'

'My maid found out.'

'Your maid told you? Chum, are you serious?'

'Yes.'

I could see him thinking for a moment.

'Okay, well I don't know what you're talking about,' he said, 'I don't know about any of this, I only moved into the place at the end of October, but I was never told about any armed burglary. No one mentioned it.'

'Oh, right.'

'In fact, the people I bought it off kept telling me how safe it is around here. All this jazz about neighbourhood watch patrols and stuff, but no one mentioned anything about a burglary.'

He looked annoyed, but not with me. I thanked him, he strolled off. Lined along the one side of the driveway was a winding hedge, tall, thick. Along the other side, next to the wall, was an abundance of luscious shrubs, small, full bushes. All ample cover for figures to lurk behind, hide in. Gazing at all that greenery, even in broad daylight, would never reveal what it was concealing. I thought of our property. Dad was right and we were safer for it.

I RODE ONTO CLAIREWOOD. It was mostly uphill, it was hot. No. 5 was a property half the size of ours. A low fence with light creepers growing along it, a small manual gate padlocked with a thick chain. The garden was overgrown with short, spindly trees, dark, overhanging, maybe moss grew here, water ran somewhere. The whole of Clairewood was hooded with tall overlapping jacaranda trees, tunnelling it in dappled shadow. Even so I could see up the dirt driveway to the outline of a neat square house, a prefabricated carport, the backend of a beige Nissan Sunny. I stood for some time, looking in, wondering what had happened here, how it all unfolded, whether that same toxic atmosphere had been strung over everything.

I rattled the padlock and chain a few times. Eventually a big-boned maid appeared round the back of the house, standing at the top of the driveway, hands on her hips. She ambled down.

'Hello,' she said.

'Is the boss or the madam here?'

'The madam lives here. Mrs Willows.'

'Could you call her? I need to speak to her. Please, it's very important.'

She disappeared for ages, then came jangling a bunch of keys. I pushed my bike up the driveway, resting it against the carport. The maid stood by the front door, waiting to usher me in. There was a poky hallway with a dusty, old world smell. The pictures in ornate gild frames were tarnished, the oversized furniture dated. It reminded me of my Grandma's flat before she died.

'Izzie?' someone called.

The hallway led into a lounge where an old lady with snow white hair sat in a wing-backed armchair. She seemed very small in that broad-shouldered chair, her bones bowed, her body curled up. She had a fine papery face, pale, sunken eyes. The purple-bluish skin on her arms was inked with blotches, hanging slackly off her thin frame.

'Hello,' I said. 'I'm very sorry to disturb you.'

'Yes young man?' she said, a hard Rhodesian accent.

'I was just wondering whether I could speak to you about something that happened to my family two weeks ago?'

'*Ja?*'

'Something we may have in common. It's to do with a robbery. My family were held up at gunpoint.'

She shifted stiffly, shot through with this sudden tension, lowering her eyes on the wall behind me. She sighed, but she may have been inhaling too, bracing herself.

'And what do you want to know?'

'I'm trying to see whether we can catch the culprits, whether they're the same people who robbed you. The police haven't been much good, but if we can link the two attacks together it may help a bit.'

'I see. You're a boy playing at cops and robbers? Hey? Tell me what difference it'll make? The event you talk about has happened, hasn't it? It's in the past. You can't undo what's already taken place, can you?'

'I guess, but I'm just trying to help. It's a bit stressful at home.'

'How old are you boy?'

'I'm thirteen and a half.'

'Thirteen. A mere child. You know what I was doing when I was thirteen? I was a farm girl on my Pa's farm in the Cape, in South Africa. You know the Cape? I used to churn butter, darn my Pa's socks, make jams and preserves. Well, it was a different era. Look, you're young, you're an innocent child. You don't want to start getting all involved in things of this nature at your age, trust me.

You're going to grow up soon enough, boy, and see for yourself anyway.'

I stood in silence, but she could see I wasn't going to be so easily dispatched. She sat back.

'Okay, so what is it you want to know? Why are you so curious? Most of us want to run away from those horrible things, try erase them.'

'Well, it's not really me. I was locked in my room for most of it, but you see it's my sister, she's gone into a kind of depression.'

She gestured with some urgency so I sat on the edge of a hard, lumpy couch, the floral fabric worn and faded. I kept my eyes on the threaded outline of a petal, pale rose and biscuit grey, because now I was fearful of looking at this old woman, knowing she might reveal something about my own family I was dreading.

'Oh no, not your sister. No, no, no.'

'Yes, she's finding it a bit tough to get over,' I said.

'How old is she?'

'She's eighteen.'

'No, terrible. Truly terrible. Poor, poor girl.'

I wanted to ask if the men who had attacked her were wearing blue overalls, but already her bony shoulders had crumpled, her face too. Tears were streaming down her cheeks, her shallow chest heaving. She was swaying, back and forth, her torso moving in a slow, steady rhythm, remembering it all through her bones, the momentum bringing the image of it all in front of her again. Like that blue I'd seen at the keyhole, she was trying desperately to rid it from herself, cast it from her mind.

I RODE HOME UNEASILY, as if some blunt hard object had wedged into my shoulder blades. Freewheeling downhill under that strut of jacaranda trees, I thought over what had been said, the implications. I couldn't kid myself forever. The look on that old lady's face was the expression now cast in stone across Becca, and it was so sad that my sister looked old, much older than she was. Not a girl churning butter in the sun, but a woman of this cruel world.

I TORE UP THE DRIVE, dropped my bike by the front door, let myself in through the gridded gate, scarpering to my room. I punched in the pin for my phone and removed myself from the WhatsApp group, deleting all the posts in quick swish. In my cupboard I dealt clothes in all directions, bringing out that stashed copy of *Hustler*, rolling it into a tight tube. I took off to the kitchen, stopping briefly to scoop up a gas lighter. Behind the garage, standing over the rusty old petrol drum, I began to tear at the pages of the magazine, ripping the glossy sheaves from their spine. When I had a clutch of them, I flicked at the gas lighter, marrying the flame to the corners of the pages, watching it take hold in an arching blue swathe. Dropped into the drum, the pages fast crinkled into cindered black specs. I tore more out, lit them, dropped them. Big breasts blazed, slips of vaginas, pouting faces, golden flashes of flesh. I watched it all burn, the heat of the fire rising against my skin, the smoke pressing against the back of my throat.

I HAD A SMALL WISP of soft dark black hair spurting in spiky silken strands at the base of my penis. I'd been cherishing their growth all year since they first splintered through, cultivating them with a mustered willpower. But I stood in the locked bathroom, naked now, looking down. I'd slipped a disposable razor from Mom and Dad's en suite. I pooled warm water in the basin, lathered up a cake of soap, foaming it in my hands, pasting its whipped white froth round my crotch. I peeled the plastic sheath from the razor head, lowered it to my pubes. It was prickly, the soap parting as the blade ploughed. I didn't want this black mark of manhood creeping onto me, and the crudeness that would follow it.

I STOOD BY THE OPEN DOOR in my room, eavesdropping on sounds from Becca's bedroom, honing in on her from a guilty distance. I needed to know for sure, confirmed to me at last, what I was now convinced had happened to her. Mom was there too, but I couldn't hear anything more than the raised hushed ends of questions followed by the briefest heart-stopping utterances in reply. Their whispering infuriated me, compelling me instead to fill in the blanks, make up what I imagined was being said purely to satisfy my suspicions. I was busy constructing an entire soundtrack of aimless dialogue, random soundbites, figuring that at least this way I was part of their dialogue, a participator in the sorry affair of my ailing sister, even if I was just a mere snoop at the door.

ALREADY MY MATES had added me back to the WhatsApp group, a new video clip waiting to be downloaded. I tapped on the 'edit' button, pressing on the red minus sign to delete myself again.

SMOOTH AND HAIRLESS I might have been, but my usual night time erection hadn't stopped. It came despite my itchy red shaven pubes. It was mystifying, how my cock just hardened, jutting out like that, rearing up of its own design. Like a little independent being of its own becoming, it was flexing its muscles, strutting about, testing the waters. It was late and I was lying listening to the droll night sounds, the settled murmur about the dim pulsing house, the purling stagnations. At the point when my mind fell into that numb, neutral state a few blanking moments before sleepy abandonment, I felt the stirring begin, dragging me back to consciousness, then pulling me down into this seedy sexual underworld. The warmth rose, spreading slowly from my midriff. No, I told myself, don't do it.

THE FOLLOWING DAY I walked towards Matthew Chambers with intent, passing him with this hard, contemptible stare in my eyes.

'Hey Walker, what the hell do you think that is?'

I was already hurrying off.

'Hey, Walker, come here,' he shouted. 'Now!'

I knew he would come for me so I paced nervously round the outside of my registration class, ignoring my friends. Sure enough once the first bell sounded, his gate duties concluded, I saw him heading up the corridor.

'Walker, get to the Com,' he said. 'Move it!'

I breathed deeply and made my way quietly, strangely confident for a small junior about to be mauled to pieces. Sure I had just cause, an understanding of integrity on my side, I was pushed through the messy prefect's lounge into an enclosed quadrangle, their notorious domain, the centre of all kinds of rumoured punishments, inflictions of brutal seniority.

It was empty. Chambers ordered me to the far corner, past a square of patchy grass, along a paving of bricks.

'Do you want to tell me what that was all about?' he began.

I looked at him, emboldened ever further by this dense

feeling of rightness. I was biting down hard, the strain in my jaw beginning to mount.

'Well? Answer me you little shit.'

He was staring back, his eyes fixed with an authoritarian rage, but I was looking through it, instead searching for answers to questions of my own.

'You think you can show disrespect like that? Hey? Learn to show some fucking respect towards your seniors. Who do you think you are? Get down and give me twenty.'

I dropped to the coarse bricks and started the press ups. The hard sole of his leather shoe crunched down on my shoulder blades, a concrete block against my back. His foot administered a flat pain across my spine. But I was determined to see him off, gritting my teeth, pushing up against him with this strength I somehow mustered in my forearms. Two, three, four, five, six. His foot eased off me, the pressure dissolving. Seven, eight, nine, ten. I stopped, knowing he wasn't watching over me any longer, that cruel intimacy between us had ceased. I squatted on my haunches, he was nowhere to be seen. The quad was empty, just brick, a snatch of grass and me in the corner. The bell for the beginning of the first lesson was sounding overhead as I made my way back towards the Com lounge. The other prefects were chattering, moving on with their books to classes, and Matt was there but he wasn't joining in the banter. He was amongst them, but completely adrift, this stony look on his face, his head lowered. As I stepped into the lounge, he pushed his way through the group, eager to make a swift departure.

AT HOME I CAUGHT MYSELF eavesdropping again, but when someone came up the passage I hurried towards my bed, fanning the illusion of a self-absorbed bore.

'Danny,' Dad said, poking his head into my room, 'come and give me a hand with something please.'

'Sure Dad,' I said with mock surprise.

I was busy tuning myself evermore to the peculiarities of Becca's manner, aspects of her disposition. I was obsessively recording observations, drawing unqualified conclusions, growing alarmed at the slightest spike in her fluctuating moods. If she displayed any tetchiness, succumbing to a weepy moment, then in response I knew to expect the onset of my stomach cramps. I let them happen without resistance, only right I felt some degree of discomfort. I continued to note her intake of food, examining what she left. When she barely touched her meals, a swelter of panic overcame me. She was at risk of becoming a breathing skeleton, wasting away before our eyes, before we could save her. The frequency of when she washed her hair was a telling indicator too. Limp and greasy equalled touchy and lethargic. Mom spent ages encouraging her to get up, sitting in the lounge grooming her hair, tying it up with colourful bands while Becca sat there silent and compliant, but within minutes of Mom turning her back she'd pull it all out again. The recurrent arrival of friends buoyed her for a while, but was followed by a major slump in demeanour. She surrendered to a period when there was this sort of non-person heaped about our house, some inward, inexistent, inherent, in-being thing, as if her solid insides had all liquefied, she was this floppy water-bottle.

But later that day as I skirted up the passage, slowing as I passed her bedroom, there was the gift of a small revelation. The curtains were open, a warm wash of late afternoon sun, bright white light, lifted everything from that stale leaden gloom. Her bed had been made, a fresh duvet cover pulled smooth and hand pressed over her mattress, her pillow covers propped up. I stood in her doorway, basking in the transformation, wondering if this marked a turning point, the tacit beginnings of a recovery. I felt relaxed, as if I could breathe a bit easier in this fresh air, because I had already reached a promise with myself to suffer alongside my sister, make right by her, share in her pain.

AS A CRUEL JOKE, it was hard again, lying flat, stiffened against my tight underwear, throwing me off guard with an early evening appearance, throbbing to the point of discomfort, but I didn't allow myself to creep away to my room or lock myself away in the bathroom to free it, touch it, stroke it out. I had to be strong, I told myself, to fight it off.

BECCA APPEARED TO BE DOING BETTER that night. She was up and about, taking a regular bath, dressing herself in casual clothes. She'd even eaten a small meal and was sitting in the lounge where we were all watching TV, the Walker family, our quartet reunited. We plastered our faces with happy expressions, or at least neutral contented ones, drawing energy from the bleary commotion of the TV. We watched a UK game show, followed by an American sitcom, a reality cookery competition, all afraid to move, to shatter this perfect illusion, the notched-up volume stirring communal enthusiasm, reeling in the detachment of four separately wandering minds, making us make an effort.

ALONE IN BED I was at my most vulnerable, the mercy of weakness, those earlier unsated impulses returning. I tried tucking my hands behind my back, gritting my teeth. When I got stinging pins and needles up my arms, I turned on my side, drew my legs up to my chest, pushing my cock between them to try suffocate the shaft to softness, stem the blood flow. This was futile, a miscalculation, because instead the pressure against me or the slightest friction of my thigh against it set off a slow current of involuntary pulses in a rapid spasm, causing an ejaculate of a cold acidy slew against my legs. I scrunched the bed sheets up in a tight fist, stuffing them into my mouth, biting on them in a spontaneous moment, eking out the last milliseconds of writhing pleasure, then muffling my guttural shouts of shameful anguish. I punched the padded surface beneath me with clobbered fists till my wrists hurt.

A MESSAGE FROM AMY ARRIVED with a chime on my phone. It said, 'Hey Dan havent seen u 4 ages!! Just wanna make sure you're okay??!!' I chucked it aside and turned over, still hot with self-loathing in the aftermath of that orgasm, not long before my stomach would start running.

EARLY IN THE MORNING I withdrew that small yellow razor from where I kept it stashed in the drawers of my desk and snuck it into the bathroom so I could be sure to keep up my practice of being cleanly shaven, to keep goodly, childlike. I lathered up my pubes, scraped away at my patch of prickles, alarmed at how soon the hair had started to come back, denser, thicker. Still I swiped across it with that swooshing blade, lopping off their tiny black heads by the dozen. Already the razor blade had become hopelessly blunt, requiring more pressure to achieve the same result. I pressed too hard, my hand slipping off the shaft, turning the blade inwards, digging into my skin. Instant sharp pain stabbed at my abdomen. A trickle of blood began to ooze. I stood looking at my bleeding self in the mirror for quite some time. Then, with no real premeditation to do so, I began to repeat in a rhythmic mock-hypnotic tone the same breathless mantra again and again, 'I will not have bad thoughts about girls, I will not have bad thoughts about girls, I will not ...'

BACK IN MY ROOM I felt ill, not the usual stomach cramps, but a feverous headache, cold to the bone.

'Mom,' I called, as she passed by my door, 'I'm not feeling well.'

She came in, pressed her hand to my brow.

'Crikey Dan,' she said. 'You're burning up.'

She went out, returning with some Panado and a cup of boiling water with squeezed lemon in it. I swallowed the pills, drank the sour hot concoction compliantly, then lay back, thinking this was what I needed, some individual care and attention, a good rest. I didn't want to go to school, the awkwardness of facing Matt at the gate, my friends disbelieving ridicule when I told them I didn't want to belong to their secret group anymore, the possibility of running into Pastor Andrews around any given corner. Instead I took to my bed thinking I was going to be indulged as I'd been longing to be, but after that initial dispensing of medicines, no further hand of a white angel appeared again to anoint me from above, soothe my muggy brow, warm my chilled joints. Mom just sent Petra in most of the time to dose me with cough syrup, place a tray of chicken soup, a chunk of a buttered bread roll on my lap.

'How are you Mr Danny?' she would ask.

'I'm fine, thanks Petra.'

'You feeling better Mr Danny?'

'A bit.'

Later in the day when Dad came home he sat with me for quite a long time. We had not been alone together very much in the past couple of weeks, and now, at certain moments, his lungs filled, I was sure he was about to turn to me, look me straight on, tell me his painful, long-held secret, father to son, an exhalation of a single burden borne for far too long. But he didn't, not quite, not really. It seemed as if what happened to Becca was never going to be spoken about, given a name, or brought into the light of day.

A low, plummeting feeling settled over me, a terrible despondency. I was yearning to know something of my family's anguish, but had been cut off from everything, forcibly removed from their haunting experience, the epicentre of which stood my sister. I just needed someone to sit me down, tell me the brutal truth, speak the word itself, allow me to grapple with its concrete affirmation. Yet I was left floating about the periphery of this amorphous black mass of half-truths, white lies, padded sensibilities.

WHEN I WAS THREE OR FOUR I remember eating dinner at the table, barely seeing over the table top, even on my raised cushion. Food was still a conundrum in my life, Mom coaxing me to eat a spoonful of peas, raising the spoon above her shoulder, saying, 'Right, open wide, here comes a choo-choo train.' Other times she would declare that no one could leave the table until I had eaten three more carrots or five more beans, so my family would sit watching me with mock impatience, frowning clown-like, until a sense of unbearable pressure mounted.

After dinner Becca and I would each go for a bath in turn, then sit in the lounge in our pyjamas, sometimes the fire crackling close by in deep winter. Becca had plaits in her hair, often they shone, and her face shone too in the firelight. I used to hate having my hair washed, except when

Mom used Johnson's Baby Shampoo because the fright of an eyeful of stinging soap was miraculously negated by that gentle balm, soft on the scalp. She would knead it in, I would close my eyes to her touch, feel her fingers dipping into me.

I would crawl round on the carpet, or often out on the slate tiles of the veranda, infantile notions of this still body of water lying beyond. Dad would sit with his legs slightly apart, the game being for me to wiggle through before he snapped his knees together. Often I would be caught there, extended within his long bony legs, strung up, readied for the most excruciating torture of tickling and playful slapping, my young nerves writhing under his jibbing fingers. I would yelp and cry, sometimes he tossed me right over, Mom and Becca spinning in a loop, bringing me to land again on the lush carpet at his feet. With everything inverted, the ceiling took on this improbable realm of flightless fancy, with endless, unreachable possibilities, an entryway into a land of fantasy, as if beyond that white ceiling some other warm world lay I truly believed I'd reach, become a part of.

'DANNY ARE YOU OKAY?' I heard Mom say, standing at my door. 'You seem very down today my boy.'

'I'm fine,' I said.

'Are you sure? Nothing worrying you?'

'No, everything's okay.'

TIRED OF BEING IN MY HOT, STUFFY ROOM I went rummaging aimlessly about the house, finding myself locked in the bathroom. I dropped my clothes, sat on the edge of the bath. I had sneaked another disposable razor and held its fresh blade close to my face, turning it round in

169

my fingers. I could tell it would cut soft flesh, very easily if angled right. I lowered it to my penis, its soft shaft squeezed between thumb and forefinger, stretching the pale white skin tight. I could slice into it, draw blood, maybe if I carved all round it was possible to hack it off entirely, be done with it for good. Hovering the razor towards that silken skin for a bit, my hands began to tremble. I could cut into my scrotum, picturing an impressive flow of thick claret blood, and let it all drain out, all the filth, but I winced at the thought of that particular pain. I settled instead for the soft skin at the very top of my right thigh, angling the blade inwards, pressing it into myself. Instantly the skin broke, my flesh pierced, blood presenting itself in a silent sedated line. I knew it was coming, my nerves anticipated it, waiting on the verge of quivered fright for first contact with that cold, alien intrusion. The sting was intense, growing out across my thigh, my leg beginning to throb, but there had been no hesitation. This was the pain I was seeking, a clean pain, at last giving definition to that wrap of numbness, there at the very edge of guilt. I felt I'd acted out of brotherly solidarity, attempting to surrogate the violation on my sister by bearing this intrusion into my own body, somehow brace her from the overpowering force of her tormentors. I held it against my skin again, drew a fresh cut, a little below the first, this time chanting to myself, 'I will not have bad thoughts about girls, I will not have bad thoughts about girls, I will not …'

BACK IN MY ROOM, two plasters over the wounds, I found myself added back to the WhatsApp group. Again I deleted it. Then another message arrived from Amy wanting to know how I was, saying she was missing me. I thought of what some people had said about her, that she could be a bit easy, a bit frisky. I recalled her hand on my stomach, caressing my abdomen, my chest. I wondered if she had really wanted to move it down, slide it into my swimming briefs, slowly jack me off, maybe even lower those glossed apple-cherry lips to me? I ran my fingers over the two plasters, pressing down to rekindle the pain. It served up an explanation of what I was guilty of, what I had done to lead those three monsters into our home, to the bed of my sister. I typed, 'Hey, I'm not interested, stop messaging me, slut!!' But thank God, my finger hovering over the 'send' icon, I realised I was being stupid, unfair, illogical. Poor sweet Amy. I deleted it all and just typed, 'Hey, I'm cool, thanks, and u?'

SHE DID COME TO ME a few times later on in the evening, my mother. That's all I really longed for right then. I was probably better sooner than I let on.

I WENT TO SCHOOL ON FRIDAY and passing Matt at the gate was surprised to realise there wasn't any residual hostility between us. All I'd anticipated flaring up again simply didn't stir. In that odd aborted exchange a couple of days ago, whatever it did or didn't amount to, we had finished everything we needed to.

'Morning Sir,' I said.

'Walker,' he replied, a brief nod to me.

But when I got home from school later, at lunchtime because Mom had written to excuse me from the cricket match, I saw his silver Golf GTI parked in the driveway. The Hilux was also there.

'What's Matt doing here?' I asked.

'He wanted to come over and have a chat with Dad,' Mom replied.

'Oh,' I said.

'I think just give them some space when we go in, okay?'

'Okay.'

I crept inside, gently dropping my school bags beside the half-circular table in the hallway. I intended to sneak into the kitchen undetected, but crossing the passageway I couldn't help glancing through the lounge out onto the veranda where I could see Matt and Dad sitting. Dad had drawn his chair close, and was resting a hand on Matt's shoulder as they talked. Matt was wearing his full formal uniform, his black senior's trousers, his Colours blazer, as if he'd intentionally smartened up despite it being another scorcher of a day. His head was slightly lowered, gazing at the floor, while Dad spoke. I couldn't hear very much, but Dad sounded as if he was saying it was okay, okay to be confused and afraid, okay to feel cowardly because he was feeling cowardly, too, the whole time. It was odd, a little unnerving. I had never heard Dad speak in that tone before, with that degree of stripped back vulnerability, somewhere approaching the centre of what was the raw awful truth.

I went into the kitchen, poured myself a glass of guava juice from the fridge. Petra had made me lunch, a ham roll which she'd left covered with a mixing bowl to keep the flies off. I wasn't hungry. I stepped back into the passageway and saw that Matt and Dad had come into the lounge and Matt was giving Mom a big hug. She was holding him tightly towards her. I caught Dad's eye, signalling it was fine for me to join them.

There was a huge bouquet of pale pink roses wrapped in cellophane which lay on the dining room table. Pinned to it was a white envelope which simply said 'BECCS'.

Mom was whispering to him, 'Just give her some time, and then come and see her. She'll understand how this has been for you too.'

He kept repeating that he was sorry, so sorry, over and over again. He even said it to me too, giving me a rigid half-embrace. His face was stony but I could see it was fortified against a brace of tender emotions pushing up behind it. It was exactly how I felt, but I was determined not to begin crying in front of him. And then he left, a brief stop in the hallway as he glanced down the passage to Becca's closed door, perhaps tying to fathom the quietness and stillness which lay behind it. We were probably both suffering from the same dull and constant pain, the lingering agony of an unanswered, unreturned love.

I HEARD BLEEPING coming from down the passage very late into the night. Four sharp digital bleeps punctuating my light sleep, rousing me from the vague impression I'd been dreaming. A door opened, light footsteps treaded cautiously down the passage. It was Dad, his gait marked firmly in my mind, an appeasing counterpoint to any rising sense of danger. He passed swiftly into the kitchen, the skin of his moist feet smooching against the ceramic tiles. Then the slow unlocking of the back door, the wrought iron security grate. He was trying to work the handle back as quietly as possible, but the clang of one iron bar against another still rang out, a crude disturbance to the static night, followed by the shuffling agitation of the dogs alert in the courtyard. He whistled to them quietly, then a scuffle of paws and footsteps trailed off swiftly into this teeming silence. I wondered where he was in relation to the house, which part of the yard he was stooping. I pondered fleeing my stuffy room to follow him out, join him in his patrol, his stoic watch of our home and family. I sat up, flung the bed covers. I leant forward, brushing the taut lighted curtain away from the window. It was bright outside from the sprawl of security spots, a bleak, industrial glare. The texture of the light radiated a false warmth, a glower of uneasy heat. The blackness shone, but in a forced, synthetic manner. The shapes of the slanted roof and squat house, the sleek tarmac slip of the driveway, the desecrated yard, the far fortressed wall, were all arrested in the grip of something hard or permanent, some ceaseless interrogation. Only when my eyes had adjusted to everything that lay within this spread, its brash opaqueness dissolving, did I see the figure of my father by the wall, outlines of the dogs sniffing and trailing their noses to the ground. Dad was shirtless and barefoot but the leather holster and belt of his gun was slung over his shoulder. He was walking looking up at the wall, inspecting the coils of barbed wire, subjecting it to the fiercest scrutiny. He stopped in front of the gate, studying it for a while, poised stiffly before it, readying himself for someone to peel it back, come leaping over the top. I watched him as he watched that black space, a portal that could open on the outside, an even darker more impenetrable stretch of black night. He was not moving, just staring, absorbing what lay beyond, or casting out his senses, prying both ways down the street. He stood poised for a long time, several dead minutes. Then he dropped to his haunches, his head lowered. The dogs came bounding up to him, muzzling their snouts against his body, but he didn't respond. I could see he was breathing heavily, his lungs filling and exhaling, as if he'd just returned from a swift jog round the block. And then he swiped his hand across his brow, swabbed the trail of sweat collected in his hands between his fingers. He flicked it away. I too then felt the sweat trickle down my temples, the sudden sodden discomfort of my armpits as I let go of the curtain, collapsing back on my bed, a desperate provocation against this

174

stifling incubation, a smothered helplessness, the constitution of all I'd seen blurring almost immediately into the lull of sleep, fusing into the contorted beginnings of an already indistinct, yet somehow anxious dream.

SATURDAY MORNING. I stood in the bathroom naked, the just-used razor resting on the basin. There was a constant stinging rash on my pubes, one hot red welt. I was chaffed, scabbed, burning, looking into the mirror and saying to my sorry self, after I had cut into my flesh again, this time on my left thigh producing a neat, narrow line of leaky blood, 'I will not have bad thoughts about girls, I will not have bad thoughts about girls, I will not ...'

I MOPED ABOUT for the rest of morning, unsettled, then ridden through with this low-grade nervousness, deeper and more despondent than before. Becca remained closeted in her misery room, the door shut all the time, sealing away the vibe of fraught energy that normally diffused outwards from that space. I needed the feel of that emission, no matter it originated in a whirlpool of sustained despair. I needed it transmitted in order to calibrate my own dejection, even at irregular frequencies as I came and went about my own contrived business, to know my sister still existed. And to know we all had a purpose, a calling, a gravitation towards her state of being. Whenever she closed herself away for any extended period of time, I was wracked with an illogical fear she'd slip away from us entirely, that unobserved, unattended, her breath would at some point narrow and slow, then stop altogether. Or whenever she went for a bath, I obsessed about her lying there, stillness in the room, maybe the intermittent hollow drip of water, a pale naked girl with slashed wrists lying limp and lifeless in a blood red bath. None of her loyal friends came calling that morning. I thought maybe Matt would brave a visit, but he didn't. Once or twice I heard Mom gently pry open her door, just a foot or two, easing her head in to make discreet observations. When she did this instant tension rendered through my body, straining every one of my senses to be sure I could detect and decipher her determination. Most likely she was, as usual, drugged and drowsed. Occasionally I'd hear Mom softly call out, ask if she was alright, if she needed anything, and if lucky I'd hear a murmured grunt of a response, sometimes even just a shuffle of her body on the bed, the measured beating blades of her fan, but at least it was something I could clutch onto, bringing me a moment's relief.

DAD INSISTED WE PLAY TENNIS in the afternoon even despite it being another boiling day. He said we needed to get out the house, even if I hadn't been too well of late. Mom encouraged us, telling us not to worry, that we should enjoy ourselves. She said she'd stay at home with Becca because Aunty Jacks was coming round to spend the afternoon with them. At the club we played several sets, mixing in with the other members, but even on court I found I kept looking towards the entrance gate between points, when we crossed the net at the change of serve, wondering whether Amy would arrive. I was on edge about it, bothered by more than just the soaking rays of sun. These vacillating images of Amy's broad smile, her wavy hair, her curved chest, those long legs in a short tennis skirt, kept pressing at me. This was one place I couldn't feign an excuse towards her or ignore her. It made me glum, sullen, even nervous. I was overthinking why I should find her arrival so unsettling, a confusing muddle of limp arguments, half-baked claims.

She never came. Towards the evening Mom messaged asking us to buy pizzas on our way home because Uncle Rob had stopped by and they were now staying for dinner. She was too tired to make anything, she said. Dad was chuffed with this news, something of a licence to stay out a bit longer. He even had a few beers and bantered with some of the other men, the wit and humour sparking with the ease of old, as if some frayed motor at the back of his throat had been stripped and rewired, energising him after all these days and weeks. I sat watching him, sucking on the neck of a bottle. Was he forgetting what had happened? I was discreetly pressing on the plasters of those two cuts either side of my thighs through the fabric of my tennis shorts, my knees pulled up close to my chest, provoking the wounds to issue up a thin sting, absently thinking the thrilling memory of the blade against my skin would soothe me, focus me. But instead my raw pubes just burnt with hot irritation.

WE STOPPED OFF at Sam Levy's Village, going into Antonio's to place an order. It was stuffy inside the small takeaway, the wood-fired oven wavered with this bright volcanic red heat, so I told Dad I was going to wait outside along the promenade where there was a stretch of mani-cured lawn interspersed with rows of palm trees. Sprinklers were scattering scuds of water across the grass. I watched it arc and twist through the faint globed lamps that lined the sides of the paths, weaving the briefest spectrum of shim-mering colour the moment before plummeting. I stood looking in at the window of a large shop, seeing my own gangly reflection staring back at me, a touch distorted in the wide sheen of glass, a black discoloured mirror.

Out the corner of my eye I noticed one of the Village security guards lingering on the edge of the garden, lurking in the shadows under the canvas overhang of a shop. He materialised from the depths of this completely dark recess, or else he'd been there for ages, all day maybe, and was now this silent observer to my lowly, private actions. Something about him caught my eye, saturated in outline and focus, and I saw he was wearing one of those blue uniforms, holding a black truncheon, a cap pulled low over his face. Registering the blue triggered an immediate reaction, something I couldn't help. A mixture of images rushed me, but more than anything it was the blue mixed with the darkening light combined with the person wearing it, the indistinct black face, the eyes hooded in the long shadow of a cap. I didn't know if he was specifically watching me, he didn't do anything, he didn't react. But he was close by, standing tall and superior and threatening, seeming to face me head on, a palpitating spectre in a blue uniform.

Thoughts were coming, this fulsome darkness covering everything all of a sudden, as if someone had flicked a switch and the last of the day's light had instantly been snuffled out. I was in a darkened room, an intruder was trawling about me, ever so slightly distant from me, perhaps beyond a wall, the other side of a thin door, stooping this tunnelled slip of darkness.

AT HOME THE GENERATOR WAS CLATTERING in the courtyard, belching black channels of smoke, so it was just as well we stopped off for takeaways, Dad said. In the lounge my aunt and uncle were on good form. Becca had been eased out of her room and was propped up on the couch, sitting next to Aunty Jacks who clasped one of Becca's hands in hers, sipping a glass of chilled white wine. Uncle Rob was holding court, squatting on the small polished mahogany carved stool by the fire place, clutching a beer bottle, doing his crazy rip-offs of vacuous celebrities, pompous colonial Englishmen, fat cat crony politicians. Everyone was laughing.

'Here're the pizzas Mom,' I said, piling them up on the long low coffee table.

'O Danny boy,' Uncle Rob started singing in a thick African accent, his eyes puffed out, blowing air into his cheeks to fatten them, 'da marimbas they be ca-ll-ing!'

I always giggled at this clowning pantomime routine. Aunty Jacks rolled her eyes, saying, 'Oh just ignore the old tart darling, and come give your favourite aunt a big kiss.'

I dished out plates to everyone and we peeled back the pizza boxes, all tucking into a fat slice. Even Becca wanted one. The aroma of melted cheese and grilled garlic filled the room, the cheery festive mood uplifting, the six of us gifted with what seemed this momentary elevation into a flighty world of cool skies, thin air, the freshness of dew misting against the skin. There was a feeling of lightness about us all, reminding me of those Easter holidays in the mountains, especially the freedom of the small mountain apes we'd watch from the balconies of our cottages on the slopes, swinging from branch to branch, picking berries and wild fruits, sometimes brazenly snatching food from plates left out on the terraces, that weightless absence of worry. What my Granddad called *skelem bobojans* or naughty monkeys. I ate five big slices of pizza all by myself, not a care in the world. I watched Becca closely. She managed two!

IT WAS ONLY towards the end of the evening when Aunty Jacks and Uncle Rob were saying their goodbyes in the hallway that I picked up on something which slashed a hole in our cautiously pitched carefree mood.

179

As he was walking out the door, I heard Uncle Rob whisper to Dad, 'everything alright, Mike, bucks wise?'

Dad shrugged his shoulders. 'Cash flow's getting a tad tight here and there,' he said, 'but we're holding up.'

'Let me know if I can tide you over. Don't be too proud to ask,' Uncle Rob said.

'Thanks mate.'

It was the first time I had heard any mention of money problems. It hadn't occurred to me, but I realised it must've been a considerable sum Dad had lost, all that money he'd been paid out for his share of the business sitting there in the safe. It must have been tens of thousands at least. What were we living on?

Then Dad said, 'but if I need a loan I'll just go and tap our good honest chum, Julius Sithole. I'm sure he's got the odd tidy stash that just happens to be sitting about.'

Uncle Rob chuckled, shaking his head. 'That fucking cunt,' he breathed to Dad, not in his usual jocular way, but with genuine hostility, bitter hate, and they lifted their eyebrows at one another, exchanging knowing glances.

IN THE MIDDLE OF THE NIGHT there was a presence in my room, a tall slender weight hovering at the end of my bed. I turned in the loose grip of sleep, sensing it more than seeing it, a constitution of matter and sentiment transcending its presence onto me like a dense formless shadow, stiff with intent.

'Danny.'

It was my father. My eyes narrowed in on him in the weak saturation of light drifting from the passage through my open door.

'Dad?'

'Are you okay?' he said.

His voice was grave again compared to at the tennis club, the pizza evening, heavy and toneless. I was more awake now, wondering whether I'd had a nightmare or something had made me shout out at random. I wondered if I'd said anything I shouldn't have, whether I'd made some wild accusation or revealed my shocking truth. Then the impression came that he'd been there for a while, nothing I could know for certain beyond this feeling he'd been in my room for some time, standing at the end of my bed, quietly looking over me.

'Yes Dad,' I said, 'and Becca?'

'Yes, she's okay.'

'And you Dad, are you okay?'

He didn't answer, his steady breathing measured out in the room, this sad drawn, downcast rhythm to it.

'Get some sleep Danny,' he said.

I LAY AWAKE ON MY BACK, the sheet discarded, the long hours till dawn cruelly ticking by. I was pressing at the wounds on my thighs again, at the same time toying with this idea, formulating this fantasy that I was back there again, at the shopping village, striding towards that guard, across the wet grass and sodden bricks, the glimmer of flying water behind me, cutting arcs in the steel night air, and I confronted him this time, coming within three feet of his face and in a low breathless rant, I said, 'I know you, arsehole, I know exactly who you are. And I'm sick and tired of you. You think you can change what you are, mingle in with the crowds? You're playing a security guard now, pretending to watch over everyone, keep people and their property safe from harm, but I know what you are. I know what you do. Where are your partners in crime, hey, your other two cohorts? Because your time has come, your blue uniform has given you away and now I've found you.'

EARLY IN THE MORNING I pulled out my bedside drawer and fished for the old cigar box I kept pressed towards the back. I ran my fingers briefly over the engraving on the front. 'TUCKETTS' sprawled in bold capitals, then slanted in this fancy curved font was the word '*Marguerite*' cased in a banner, against a background of tropical plants, a wide palm frond. The carving was intricate, the wood soft and light, always compelling me to finger it, as if reading braille, blind to some unknown past. Then I flipped it open, spreading out my savings. I had two twenties, three tens, a five. I took out a twenty and laid the rest back in the box, slipping it into the drawer.

I could hear signs of movement coming from my parents' room. Although it was Sunday, the light still firming outside, they were awake. Dad had probably been through to make them coffee. I folded up the money and went down the passage. I stood in their doorway. It was dim, the curtains were still drawn. The fan overhead whipped the air, making a slight clanking sound. But the air was still warm, even stale. Mom was lying curled up asleep on her side with Dad sitting propped up next to her but he wasn't watching TV, reading or even staring at those dull grey security monitors. He was just waiting by her side, looking down over her.

I came a few paces into the room. I was about to hand over the thirty bucks, say how I wanted to pay for the pizzas, help out a bit, even if it wasn't very much. But then I saw Mom's disarming mop of ruffled hair and under it a slip of her face, washed-out white. Her eyes were closed, her face expressionless. I glanced at Dad and he raised his finger to his lips.

'Shhh, Danny. She's been sick all night,' he whispered. 'Must've been something that disagreed with her in one of those pizzas, hey. Best just let her rest for a while.'

'Oh,' I said, 'poor Mom.'

THE HABIT TOOK HOLD QUICKLY. It was the thrill of being drawn to a daring act, the test of nerves, inflictions of pain. By now the plastic travel razor was as blunt as a piece of serrated cardboard. It scratched over my skin, barely even nicking it. With Mom sick in bed I couldn't sneak another one from their bathroom, so instead I went in search of a more elegant instrument. I banged about the garage till I found a cluttered box of empty wine bottles, at once mesmerised by their shapes, their elegance. There was a particular bottle, tall and slender, with a long graceful neck, an accentuated lip. It was cool to the touch. The glass was rich burgundy when I took it outside, held it to the sun. I could barely see through its opaqueness but it lit up in this pulsing, coppery glow. Something about it triggered a thought, a propulsion in me, the knowledge I was in the garage by design, some subterranean level of need motivating me to go in search of a truer, more worthy weapon. I cleaned the bottle in boiling water, a dab of bleach. Petra thought I was mad but I fobbed her off, telling her I was working on an art project for school. Soon it emerged with a smooth lacquered sheen and it instantly excited me. I dried it off, wrapped it in a big bath towel. I laid it on the ground back in the garage and struck it with a hammer. It capitulated after the first blow in a dull, almost soundless thud. Unwrapping it carefully, I saw it had all worked perfectly, there were five amply sized chunks, some near semi-circles with edges I knew were even sharper than razors.

I STOOD IN THE CHURCHLY SANCTUM of the bathroom, breathing deeply, wincing at the deep and delicate definition of the pain, my mind soaring in some flighty, fragmentary realm. It reminded me of that childhood delight I took in the unfathomable deeps of the white ceiling, held in my father's grip, a certain belief in the magical whiteness of clouds. 'I will not have bad thoughts about girls,' I panted, 'I will not have bad thoughts about girls ...'

SHE WAS UP BY LUNCHTIME but looked no better. Although she said the fever and vomiting had stopped, her eyes looked heavy and swollen.

'Are you okay Mom?' I asked.

'I'm fine Danny, just the flu or something. Maybe I caught a bug going around.'

She wasn't much better in the evening either, even though she'd been back to fussing about Becca again. Dad and I picked away at some leftover chicken casserole and rice from the week, sitting in front of the TV, but Mom didn't touch a thing. She just lay on the sofa next to Dad as he held her hand, slowly rubbing it with his thumb, as if quietly calming her, reassuring her. He cast a studied glance over her every couple of minutes.

I excused myself from their company, making my way down the passage. I stood in the doorway of their bedroom, tiptoed towards Mom's side of the bed first and knelt down to unclasp the buckle on her handbag. I felt for her purse, snapped it open. She had a bit of cash, perhaps fifty dollars, but she usually paid for groceries and sundries with her bank card. How much was in the account? I had no way of knowing. I crawled round the bed to Dad's side, pried open his bedside drawer. I couldn't see his wallet or anything else. Maybe he had no money in the bank at all now? Perhaps it was all gone? How were we going to pay for everything? My school fees? Becca's doctors? Carry on the way we lived? Something had to be done, I decided, to get back what we'd lost.

WHAT I DID NEXT WAS IMPULSIVE. The connections weren't logical or coherent, but during break time at school the next day I snuck away from my friends, strolled towards the remote art block and took out my cell phone. I dialled 0772835771. Something in me was determined, more than ever. The line rang off a few times but eventually he answered.

'Mr Zach, it's Daniel Walker here, I spoke to you a while back about a robbery at my house, No. 11 Alice Smith Road.'

'And?'

'Well you came to our house that night it happened. I heard you in the kitchen, talking to my Dad. You said you know everything that happens in this town. You said you work at Special Branch. You said you make the guilty pay for their crimes? That you make justice happen.'

There was silence.

'Well,' I continued, 'I need your help, I really need to find those three men who attacked us. They have stuff that belongs to us and we need it back.'

'We are looking into the case,' he said, 'it is an ongoing investigation.'

'But, sir,' I said, 'I'm sorry but that's not good enough.'

'It's procedure, you have to be patient. These things, you know, they take, how do I say it, certain resources.'

I could sense his undertone immediately, I wasn't ignorant. Without hesitation I just said, 'I'll make it worth your while, okay? I can pay you, give you some money.'

My rationale was only wafer slim, perhaps I even knew it in that very moment. What were the chances we'd find them, now? Yet I understood one thing very clearly, and it was that those intruders' freedom meant my family's imprisonment, the crude iron bars on our doors and windows, but also the hold they had on our minds, our fears and feelings. Only the reversal of this could set us free.

I heard him rolling over what I'd said, what I was offering. Maybe he was chewing gum on the other end of the line, or biting down on his teeth. Then he said, 'Okay let me see what I can do. You say No. 11 Alice Smith?'

'Yes.'

'I'll come back to you.'

WHEN I ARRIVED HOME FROM SCHOOL Mom was nowhere to be seen. In the car Dad had said she was still feeling a bit down, but I didn't expect to find she'd taken completely to bed. I crept down the passage, quietly turned the doorknob, poking my head into their room. She was lying on her side again under the thick duvet, shivering, even despite the hot weather.

'Dad,' I said, back in the kitchen, 'I think Mom's really sick. You better go and see.'

He went in to check on her. I didn't see him for another hour. There was this barrier, a hard closed door, behind it the same muted exchanges. I think I heard her crying at one point. I padded closer, the nerves in my stomach tightening.

It was Dad who attended to Becca that evening. For the first time I felt this resentment pooling towards her, thinking she was dragging this whole saga on for too long now, it was all becoming a bit pathetic. But in fairness when she heard that Mom was ill she made an effort to get up, to ask Petra what she could scramble together for us for dinner.

She sat with us in the lounge, making a concentrated effort to perk herself up, be more alert.

Later Dad said, 'I think Mom's just really worn down and tired. The last few weeks especially, they've been really tough for her. Tougher than we can imagine, hey. So I think we just need to let her rest completely till she gets her strength back, okay?'

'Yeah, of course Dad,' I said.

'Don't worry, she'll be hundreds again within a few days, you'll see. Everything's going to be back to normal soon, my boy, I promise you.'

I SENT MR ZACH A SERIES OF LONG MESSAGES detailing what happened to us. I gave him the original docket number of our case, thinking he'd mislaid it. I told him about the connections I'd discovered to Kirby Road and Clairewood, all about poor old Mrs Willows. And I told him it was extremely urgent, more so than when we spoke earlier, because it had finally all caught up with my mother, the stress, the trauma, the exhaustion, it was making her ill. I pleaded with him to help me and promised I could come up with a payment for him. I emphasised that with a series of $$$$$$ emojis, hoping he'd take the bait. 'Let me c wat I cn do,' he finally replied.

THE NEXT MORNING IN THE KITCHEN I said, 'Dad, surely Mom has to go to the doctor, she's not getting any better?'

'I've tried but she refuses,' he said, 'point blank.' He was fiddling with a bowl of Weetabix. He looked nervous himself, on edge, fretful. 'And anyway, I don't know what the doctor's going to say. I mean he's just going to tell her what we know, that she's physically exhausted, that she's overdone herself in the last few weeks and then tell her to rest.'

'But maybe it's more than that?'

'Like what?'

'I don't know, some virus or something. Or even something else. She won't stop crying. She looks terrible. There must be a reason.'

He shook his head. 'No, I don't think so hey. I think we just need to be patient and let her get back into the pace of things slowly. This is how people who are completely whacked out act Daniel. They're so tired they can't see things clearly. Everything feels a hundred times worse and more difficult than it really is. They get emotional. Women particularly.'

I sighed, turning towards the kitchen window. I didn't want him to see the thick tears welling in my eyes.

I PHONED MR ZACH AGAIN. He assured me he was working on it, but, '*ish*, these matters they take time and resources my friend, you know?' and in this pause I could imagine him rubbing his fingers together, implying what I now began to dread.

'Alright,' I said, 'we'll talk about that later. But I need to see some results first. Okay? No results, no money.'

'Guaranteed.'

'Yeah, I hope so. And I know you're probably very busy but we need to move fast.'

'I'm working on it as we speak. I've already laid some preliminary ground work. I'm tracing the files. Trust me.'

I cut the line and wondered exactly what I'd gotten myself into.

AT LUNCHTIME a white Mazda Familia, slightly dilapidated, with tinted windows, missing hubcaps and a battered spoiler came crawling into the Shell service station up the road from school, pulling to a halt in front of the kiosk.

All day I'd been aware of these two twenty dollar and one ten dollar bills burning in my pocket, spreading this uneasy dread. I couldn't see through the tinted windows of that Familia. It was stationary for a good few minutes before there was any sign of movement. I felt exposed, scrutinised from behind this sinister screen. Then the driver's window inched down on the face of a bald man, slanted sideways onto me. He was wearing dark glasses, his complexion looked a little oily, his cheeks bloated, the dome of his head very round. He raised his chin, gesturing with his hand. There were about ten paces of oil slicked concrete between us but every step I took felt instinctively untraceable, my gut tight and muscles stiff.

'Mr Zach?'

He nodded. 'Get in.'

He leaned over to open the passenger door for me. I walked round the bonnet, searching for ways to talk him out of a protracted encounter, maybe tell him it was okay, I didn't need his help after all. But then I was sitting next to him, he'd started the engine and was pulling away.

'Where're we going?'

'You're lucky I agreed to come to you,' he said, 'normally it would be you coming to me.'

'I just want to know where we're going, please.'

'The place that is a small place where the big things happen,' he replied.

'Where's that?'

He didn't answer. I felt queasy, not helped by the grubby interior of the Mazda. The grey leather seats were badly worn and sun-frayed. The dashboard was grimy, something sticky had spilt over it, dried to a streaky crust. It smelt of greasy fast food and perspiration, of something slightly off and seedy.

'Please I'm actually not very comfortable,' I said, 'doing this.'

'Just relax.'

He drove fairly slowly, his lips pursed, as if annoyed with something. I couldn't see his eyes for his shades. Despite the heat, he wore a black leather jacket which, even then, I felt was too obvious a cliché to pass as authentic. Was he trying a bit too hard to impress me, the small white kid playing a game of detectives?

I started to feel for my cell phone in the pocket of my shorts.

'You won't be needing to contact anyone,' he said, without glancing at me. 'You understand the nature of our business? That this is strictly off the books?'

I rested my hands on my lap. 'Yes, I understand,' I said.

'Good. It's good to have an understanding between people who do business with one another, isn't it?'

'Yes.'

'Yes, so now we understand. You brought my fee?'

'Yes,' I said, tapping my shirt pocket.

'That's good,' he said.

WE HEADED STRAIGHT FOR TOWN. We drove along Enterprise Road, then from Glenara Avenue we turned right onto the dual carriageway of Samora Machel, channelling us into the heart of the city. The dated high rise buildings stacked up ahead, the traffic thickened, all these people swarming about. Everything congealed together, this heaving haphazardness of organics and matter, synthesised with my nerves. There was a haze over town, this grubby shadow floating off the tops of the grey squat buildings. Commuter omnibus kombis streamed past us, stopping arbitrarily, jostling for customers, all bleating chaotically in the taut air. Town soon felt cramped, dirty concrete, struggling out-dated shops, posters of the President's face flattened over every spare inch, litter strewn on the cracked pavements.

In the depth of its guts there was a whole new atmosphere. We weaved along the dirty cramped streets, deeper into the ramshackle hovel of dilapidated buildings, potholed roads, crevices often pooled with black stagnant water. The throng of people thickened, pedestrians walking along, many lingering in the middle of a mindless day. It all gave off a fumy heat, the stench of passive misery.

'Please tell me where are we going?' I asked.

'We're going to the market.'

'The market? What market?'

'Mbare market.'

'Why Mbare market? What's there?'

'As I said, people who know things and people who see things. That's why we're going to Mbare market.'

IT WAS A HEAVING CONFUSION of shacks and black sheeted plastic stalls. The shacks were made from bendy corrugated tin, lopsided and unstable. The plastic sides of the stalls were ripped and tatty. Nothing looked very sure, it was all disorientating. I followed Mr Zach closely, conscious of how easy it would be to get lost in a maze I had no confidence of escaping. Everyone was looking at me. Vendors offered a countless array of goods, proffering merchandise under my white nose. Others stared with eyes of resentment and suspicion.

The ground was eroded asphalt, very fine red soil, clomps of rocks and stones. I kept my eyes down, watched my footing. It was hot inside and I could smell *sadza* being cooked, at times the overpowering glut of raw meat. Behind the odd shack or round a narrow twist, I glimpsed the occasional big black pot poised over a brick and mesh wire fire pit. Belches of smoke swarmed up my nose, stinging my eyes. Mostly there was a conglomeration of abject junk strewn over bendy trestle tables made from planks of mouldy pine.

Further in, everything narrowed, becoming very claustrophobic. Here the plastic sheeting was strung overhead joining all the stalls together into one dark giant canopy, only occasionally the beams of sunlight pierced through the rips, exposing the starkness of what lay beneath. I could hardly see what I was looking at and wondered at the point of it all.

Then it became clear. I began to see. Scattered all round these stalls a different kind of commodity was being traded. We were now past the touristy soapstone carvings of rhinos and elephants, the copper bangles, beaded necklaces, the bright local fabrics, piles of fake Chinese imports, the racks of pirated movies. We were now in the hi-tech department of fancy TVs, game stations, DVD players, stereos, cell phones, iPods, iPads and laptops. Nothing was packaged in a box, it all lay out, heaped about, nakedly evident. When I saw the rows of borehole motors and pumps, tarnished from use, the electric gate motors neatly snipped from their casings, the array of 12 and 24 volt batteries, all the high-spec tools and machinery, the endless clutter of car parts, I knew straight away.

Mr Zach was asking a few questions of some shady looking men. We followed someone to a small stall where there was a thin shadow of a man perched on a stool, his back to the sheeting. I couldn't make out his face except that it was framed in wiry dreadlocks and grizzly stubble. Mr Zach spoke to him in Shona. There were a few moments when was he looking at me, just as everyone was looking at me, as if they all did things in unison, by silent collaboration. There was this malign atmosphere, a brittle tension simmering under the heat and dimness of those tents, and I felt someone slink past me, brush past me in an intentional way, their body oppressive and heavy, a wisp of hot breath purposely laid on my neck.

After some negotiation the man clicked his tongue and reluctantly bent down, bringing out a tin box from under the trestle table. It was grey, narrow, rectangular, a thin padlock opened by a tiny key fished out of an unsighted pocket. He flipped the lid back on a nest of entangled clutter, sharpening into a trove of jewellery, necklaces, rings, earrings, trinkets, bracelets, brooches, strings of pearls. When I looked closer I could even make out the shimmering liquescence of stones.

'Have a look in this box,' Mr Zach said, 'and see if you can identify anything which may have been the property of your mother.'

'Okay.'

'Look carefully. Is there anything here you can recognise?'

'I don't know. I mean there's so much.'

'See if you can see anything of your mother's property.'

I BENT OVER THE TABLE, peering into the box. There was so much of it knotted and intertwined. It was impossible to decipher anything. I tried to cast my mind back to memories of Mom's jewellery, to years gone by when I remembered her wearing it. It wasn't that often she brought out the really valuable pieces, but there was the odd formal occasion when she wore her diamond earrings. They always reminded me of a flower, there was one large diamond in each of the ring's centres, then a series of smaller ones cast around it.

I scratched about in the tin a bit, conscious of its keeper's iron glare on me, but there was nothing I recognised. Mom had a string of pearls that had belonged to Grandma. They sat in a box, black velvet on the outside, slightly off white satin inside. I used to run my fingers over that box when I was small, fascinated more by the soft feel of smooth velvet against my fingers than its contents. Once when Mom had them out I was allowed to pick them up. She was sitting at her dressing table putting on make-up. She was wearing a stunning black dress.

I was sitting at her feet on the carpet pushing the box round as if it were a car when she looked down on me. 'Now be a gentleman Danny and fasten my string of pearls,' she said in a high-pitched, fake-posh accent.

I opened the box, feeling the tension in the sprung hinges flip the lid back. The pearls lay there neatly pressed into their groove. I picked them up, startled by their cool weight. I had assumed they would be like plastic beads but it felt as if I were holding a clutch of the world's finest miniature marbles. I dangled them round Mom's neck as she guided my fingers to the small gold latch. I fumbled at it a while but was determined to fasten them round her.

Afterwards she said, still in character, 'What a fine young man you are, Master Daniel Walker.'

I remember breaking down into a fit of giggles as she tickled me. Dad had just come out the shower. He had a towel wrapped round his waist. He moved in the room like a long brown shadow behind us.

194

I BRUSHED MY FINGERS over the pearls in the tin horde, briefly wondering what memories they would kindle in other victims. That they should end up here seemed an entirely different kind of theft altogether.

'No,' I said, 'I can't recognise anything really.'

'Are you sure? Look again. Look closely.'

I scratched about a bit more. There were heaps of gold rings which all looked the same to me, gold necklaces and bracelets of different thicknesses. There was one bracelet engraved with a lattice pattern. It looked vaguely familiar to something I recall Mom wearing once or twice. I held it, thumbing over the engraving. I brought it close to my eyes to see the pattern more clearly.

'This one?' he asked.

'I give you good price,' the stall keeper said.

I ignored him and held the bracelet close to my eyes.

'I don't know, maybe.'

Mr Zach was speaking in Shona again, this time more aggressively.

I slowly placed the bracelet down. Immediately the tin was slammed shut and slipped from sight in a second. The man on the stool looked away. It was as if the tin had never been there at all.

I wondered whether one of those thugs, my thugs, our thugs, was right in front of my nose or whether I was actually surrounded by any number who could well be them. How would I know? Would something still link us together, two weeks later? Some happenstance, some instinctive inner knowledge? My ears were pricked to the sound of those voices, my sense of smell narrowing. I picked up the distinct sour smell of urine and at once was back there, in my room in the dark, cupping my hands to my crotch, the sight of a blue figure captured in a keyhole.

Mr Zach's shouting grew louder. He was demanding information, but I couldn't understand.

'These men you say they were wearing blue?' he said to me.

'Um, what?'

'Blue. You said they were wearing blue clothing, yes? White boy, wake up!'

'Yes. They were. Blue overalls. Standard blue worker's overalls.'

People were moving now, they were silently slipping away, drawing further into those dark warrens. I was under no illusions anymore about where we stood, what manner of individual had been surrounding us.

The rant in Shona continued, then he had me by the arm and was pulling me along with him.

'We go now,' he breathed at me. 'Hurry, follow me. Don't look back. These people remember.'

HE LED ME OUT of the canopy where the sudden bright light made me light-headed, woozy.

'Keep your eyes on the ground now,' he said, 'try not to look at anyone.'

The hubbub of people had grown, there were vendors everywhere now. They'd seen us, heard the commotion or news had spread of what we were after, what unspoken accusation we'd made, and now they were crowding round us, goading us, as if we'd come here with the purpose of disturbing some fragile balance.

'Hey, hey, hey, white man,' one said, 'you go away.'

'Go back to your Britain,' another shouted.

'*Viva* his Excellency the President of the Republic,' a woman chanted from a distance, her fist raised triumphant in the air, 'we will never be a colony again!'

BACK IN THE CAR I sat catching my breath. Mr Zach wasted no time in pulling away, driving off at speed.

'You managed to find something out?' I asked.

'Something, yes.'

'That's good. It will help us catch them, right?'

'Yes, maybe. Maybe not.'

He drove the rutted streets for a while, weaving in and out of stuttering traffic. I hardly had time to process those thugs, that trove of jewels, the shouting, the intimidation. I had no idea what he had or hadn't unearthed. I just sat, staring at this heaving streetscape and it all seemed slightly beyond reality.

We turned into a less chaotic side road and he pulled into the first parking he saw.

'This is Kaguvi Street,' he said, and he gestured to a nondescript blistered cream-coloured building about fifty feet beyond our parking, 'and that there is Special Branch Headquarters. It's a secret place, high-level security, so you don't tell anyone I take you here, see?'

'Of course,' I said.

'Wait here, I need to go find something.'

He got out the car, disappearing down the sidewalk. People were milling about in a slow, lethargic pointlessness. I looked down at the flat two-storey building. I wondered what exactly went on in Special Branch. How many files on shady citizens they collected, persons of interest, people in high places? What top secret scandals did they keep tabs on, political intrigue, affairs of state, people of prominence, gay encounters, dodgy mining deals, acts of corruption? Then I wondered if that's what they did at all.

I looked about inside the car, opening the cubby hole. I was expecting to see the shaft of a pistol, one of those stout-handled, carbon cast ones I supposed the undercover police carried, and maybe a pair of sinister black leather gloves draped over it to go with the jacket he was wearing. But there was just a grubby tan wallet heaped amongst other bits of junk. I hesitated before picking it up and opening it, briefly filing through its contents. I was expecting to find his police ID, marked Special Branch HQ, Kaguvi Street. There were only a commonplace national identification disk. I peeled it out of its pouch and read the name 'ZACHARIAH SINGANO'.

IT WAS ANOTHER TWENTY MINUTES before he returned. I was growing anxious as it was getting on into the afternoon. He was smoking a cigarette, clutching a lime green folder under his right arm. He slid it down the side of his seat and the whole way back to the suburbs I wondered about it, what information it held.

When we were out of town I said, 'That market, Mbare, why is it that you know of all those stolen goods there and all those *tsotsis* but they haven't been rounded up and arrested?'

He was quiet for a bit, chewing over his response. 'You *murungus* don't know how this place works,' he said. 'You just need to know that you have to let some of these people function if you want to catch the rest of them. It's the same with everything.'

He gestured out the window, perhaps at the country itself.

WHEN WE PULLED IN at the service station, he opened up the folder. It was full of papers, some were yellow, some a light green, but that's all I saw.

'So I think I can round up these men,' he said.

'Really?'

'Yes. I think I have cracked your case. These people, they always get careless, they always make mistakes. They pop their smelly bodies up over the wall one time too many. Sometimes things are right under your nose. You need to decide to smell them or not. Right, so No. 11 Alice Smith?'

'Yes.'

'And this docket report seems to confirm the link between your robbery and a number of others in the area at that time.'

'Yeah I'm sure it does.'

'No. 24 Kirby, No. 5 Clairewood.'

'Yes.'

'Well these *tsotsis* you are after, it would seem Special Branch have the notes, we have the intelligence. They could be picked up any time. So okay, this is how it's going to work. You want these men brought in?'

'Yes.'

'You want to see them pay for what they have done?'

'Yes.'

'Then I can round them up, all of them. I know where they are working from. But now that I've got this red hot file in my hands, time is of the essence. They will disappear without a trace when it becomes apparent someone is onto them. So of course an operation of this nature, it's not easy, it carries associated risks, big risks.'

'Tell me what you want. I can organise it. I promise.'

'You have seen how I work, yes? I get results.'

'Yes you do.'

'Well results like this cost money. And while fifty is a fair price for a bit of spade work like today, we are talking about a more expensive operation right now.'

'Alright.'

'So you want these three men brought in you bring me three hundred American dollars. One hundred American dollars bounty for each man, including the cost of the operation, the administration charge. Okay?'

IT WAS LATE when Dad picked me up after my usual Thursday afternoon cricket practice. It was beginning to darken, the sky that heavy chrome before the last light fades. A dull security globe fixed to a long pale blue pole flickered on, the light limp and lustreless, a few stick-thin insects started to dart about it. The traffic along Fisher Avenue had thinned out almost completely when Dad finally arrived. He'd been delayed, he said, because he'd decided to take Mom to Dr Phillips after she hadn't showed any improvement at lunchtime.

'Good,' I said, 'what did he say?'

'What we expected,' he replied, with a slight shrug, 'but she should be able to get some good rest now.'

'Thank God,' I said.

The rest of the way home we said nothing. Dad seemed preoccupied, a little downcast, and I was intent not to let on about my afternoon excursion, my mind drifting in contemplation about what my next move could be, despondent at the thought of how I was ever going to come up with that money.

At home the house and the yard were a beacon of darkness. Approaching from Alice Smith we could see this glaring absence of light, a perverse alert given all that fancy security apparatus.

'What the hell?' Dad said, immediately his whole body shot through with this rigid, beating tension. 'Why hasn't that bloody Petra put the generator on?'

I saw some pointlessness to it all. Despite our best

intentions, that vast battery of security globes and spot lights still relied entirely on a power source we had no control over, that came and went, dispensed with by an arbitrary, indifferent logic. I was tense too, syphoning Dad's fright.

He sped up the drive, braking hard just in front of the garages, flinging his door open even before we stopped.

'Petra,' he yelled.

The dogs were bounding round us, but he waded through them all, kicking one out the way. It let out a short high-pitched yelp, scattering underfoot in the darkness. He hissed at it.

I clambered after him and in the court yard I could make out the small, thin figure of Petra hovering by the generator. She looked like one of those fidgety insects, pitched on an invisible axis in the air. Dad flicked at the torch on his phone and shone it at her. She cowered under the sudden intensity of it, the polished brown skin of her face glistening in the blunt light. She was grimacing, the stark wide whites of her eyes struck with panic.

'*Amai*, when did the power go off and why haven't you put the generator on?' Dad said.

'Just about half an hour. I'm sorry boss, I try but it no wanted to start.'

'What do you mean it doesn't want to start? Did you flick the DC switch?'

'Boss?'

'Never mind,' Dad said. 'The Madam and Miss Rebecca? They are alright?'

'Yes boss. I give Miss Rebecca a candle and I have been sitting with her and the Madam she is still sleeping all since this afternoon.'

'Okay.'

Dad shone the light at the glossed yellow hulk of the genny. He flicked a few switches, tapped on the fuel gauge, unscrewed the cap, angling the narrow beam of the torch inside the tank.

'No wonder,' he sighed, 'there's no bloody fuel!'

He slapped the cap down and started marching off to the garage. 'Danny, go and see how your sister and mom are while I sort this out,' he said over his shoulder.

With the torch on my own phone I inched into the dark house. The heavy outline of everything, stencilled in the wash of weak light, was hard and blunt-edged in the kitchen, very severe. I moved down the passage. I was expecting to find Becca curled up in her room but there was a glow of light wavering from the lounge. She was sitting on the couch, the candle tame and still beside her in a sconce on the coffee table.

'Hi Beccs,' I said.

'Hi Danny.' There was a generous smile across her face, and her eyes glinted liquidly in the far soft edges of the candlelight. 'How was school?'

'It was cool,' I said. 'You okay?'

'Yes,' she said, 'I'm fine, don't worry.'

'Good.'

There was a strange quietness in the room, just the distant clatter of our neighbours' generators, counterpointing this immediate awkward tension between us, something odd about her temperament, the unexpected lightness of her voice, her easy expression in the uneasy light. It caught me off guard, making me think it was all contrived, a very well-rendered deception. I studied her, glancing across her body with a careful eye, scouting for signs of damage. Was she holding Dad's pistol beside her? Had she somehow found out where he kept it? I looked at the soft gleam across her eyes and wondered if they were about to glaze over any second, roll back in her face as her body collapsed, writhing in flaccid convulsions, perhaps the result of a bag of pills down her throat?

Oh God. I breathed in. I was about to scream my lungs out for help, not even sure I had the ability to open my mouth. Then she said, still smiling, 'Mom's out for the count. She's asleep on her bed.'

THERE WAS BARELY A DULL GLOWER in the house as I walked down the passage. I treaded quietly into Mom's room, sensing her shape more than seeing her, stretched out under the slope of a light sheet, lying on her side. I could hear her breathing, deep and regular. I drew the torchlight down over her, observing her lank dark hair, plastered close to her scalp, the long strands draped like vines over her face which looked clammy and crimson. Her eyes didn't even blinker in the scour of light. I angled my phone to shine over her bedside table and picked up a packet of pills I saw lying next to a half-filled glass of water. I lowered the label to the glow. 'Hypnovel midazolam, X8, 6mg, Mrs J. Walker. Take two tablets every four-six hours or when necessary to aid sleep and acute cases of exhaustion.' I stood over Mom for a bit, looking down on her. I thought back to Becca a few moments ago in the lounge. I was certain she was concealing something, or that perhaps she was on the verge of trying something desperate. With Mom out of her way, her guardian, her guard, she had the perfect opportunity. Or maybe that was just it? Perhaps all Becca had wanted these past few weeks was to be left completely alone, just as, in that brief moment, I thought how quiet and sedate the house felt with most of that intrusive security system out of operation. Until now the attack had seemed continual, all of us in some way under siege. This was different, a dangerous peace of sorts. But then a loud clattering tattoo swept in from outside as the generator cranked up, followed a few moments later by the lights coming on. Water started to pump into the cisterns and geysers, devices across the house beeped and bleated, the grey screens by the bed started to flicker, rolling to life, but I didn't see Mom stir for an instant.

LATER, AFTER PETRA HAD FIXED us some bacon sandwiches, and Becca had gone for a bath, Dad called me into the lounge. There was a faint reek of diesel about him, some must have spilled on his clothes, and the gun was lying in its holster beside his chair again. I was curious about where exactly he did keep it, whether it was safely locked away. I couldn't help but study it rather nervously for a while and even when he told me to sit down on the couch I felt its tense presence beating out from the table.

'Danny,' he began, 'listen to me my boy. I know you've been very good these past few weeks with everything that's happened, okay, but you know it's your job around the house to make sure the genny is always topped up and you know we last used it on Saturday. The very first thing you should have done on Sunday was make sure you'd seen to it. You understand me?'

'Yes dad,' I said.

'Because I tell you, there are more of these bastards out there, and they're waiting to come. They don't like us, what we are, who we are, or what we've done in the past, and we're always going to be a target in this place. You understand?'

I nodded.

'Danny, do you? Really? Because you need to take some responsibility too and help me keep us safe.'

'Yes dad.'

'The sun may shine, my boy, but remember that we're no longer living in a paradise here.'

I WAS MORE INTENT, more directed that night. I pressed the glass to my thigh and began to cut. I felt the blade grate, begin to sink deeper. The pain was sharp and intense. But it drew me in too. My mouth tightened, my eyes focused, my wrist firmed, the weight of my hand dropping and my fingers stiffening. I knew I was cutting myself deeper than those few previous times. I pressed down harder, the glass slashing my skin, ripping into my thigh. The blood welled quickly and began to trickle down my leg. I pulled the glass away, my flesh gouged. There was a ring of stark bright blood, darkening on my skin already. I stood up straight in the centre of the bathroom, naked and tall, closing my eyes on what was sure to be a long loathsome night ahead. I was trying to coax the awful truth venting out of that hot pain to coalesce into a sense of affirmation, a belief I had at last actually determined to do something to restore my family's losses, to act against my guilt, our blame, even if it was all just a vague longshot, a cry in the vast dark. I slid the tips of my fingers through the blood pooling at the wound and then smeared it across my loins, my chest, my neck. I drew a line of blood under both my eyes.

ZACHARIAH SINGANO seemed surprised when I called him early the next day, but he told me he'd come and pick me up. This caught me off guard and threw me into a panic. I asked him why I needed to go with him, but he told me it was essential.

'You will need to come, when we bring them in, it's procedural.'

'Okay,' I said, 'but it will have to be later, in the afternoon.'

'No,' he said, 'it can only be tonight.'

'Tonight? I don't know. I mean I'm not so sure about tonight.'

'This kind of sting operation can only happen at night. Where we have staked them out, where we know they will be operating from.'

'Oh right,' I said.

'So I will pick you again from the garage.'

'No,' I said, trying to think, 'I won't be able to be at the garage.'

Instead I gave him directions to the bottle store over the hill on Alice Smith, the nearest, safest landmark I could think of. He said he would find it. I didn't have his money, of course, and a part of me knew the whole plan was improbable. I thought if I could fob him off long enough, string him along until we did catch our *tsotsis* and had recovered all of Dad's money, then I was sure he would been more than happy to slip Zachariah a backhander, his fee worth the price.

I concocted a plan to say I was staying the night with Watts, who lived in the next suburb. It was a doable distance by bike and a trip I'd made often before, especially during the holidays when always looking for things to do. Traipsing off all over the place on bike had never really caused my parents much concern, not before the attack, and I was relieved that asking to stay the night at the Watson's didn't seem to cause much anxiety, even my insistence on riding when Dad offered to drop me off.

'Just be careful crossing Churchill,' he said, 'and go before the rush hour traffic gets too thick.'

'Sure Dad,' I said.

I doubted anyone would check with Sally Watson because Mom usually did that. That sort of thing never occurred to Dad. When I set off, although Mom was up and looking calmer, somewhat rested, she wore this glazed and grinning expression, slightly disarming, but at least an assurance that the pills were making her loopy and I knew she was pretty much out of it. I hugged her goodbye and she whispered that she loved me, her eyes welling over, but I didn't say anything to her in return other than thanks and goodbye. Already I was on edge, my stomach tight and uneasy, and I tried not to convey my nerves.

I had packed a satchel. It contained some jeans, a jacket and some hardy shoes I wore when we occasionally hiked up the *kopjes* surrounding the city for picnics or sundowners. I thought that more appropriate than shorts and slip-ons. I don't know why I packed the jacket, it was far too hot for one. I slipped in a can of Peaceful Sleep mosquito repellent. I made sure my phone was fully charged and brought the little that remained of my savings from the old cigar box.

I SLOGGED UP THE HILL then freewheeled down towards the crescent where the bottle store sat. It was late afternoon, the usual settlement of layabout sellers had dwindled away. There were other people hovering about in a loose formation, an idle, festive crowd, lured by the local beer, the scuds of *chibuku*. I approached cautiously, remembering the last time I'd infiltrated these same people on that inferno of an afternoon, my manner hot and cocky. I glimpsed a fuzzy mirage of myself as I glided down towards the rippled heat of the dust bowl, the potholed tarmac which lay strewn before the stores. It was only three short weeks, but seemed a fathomless age.

They were used to me hassling them so didn't act in any hostile way to my reappearance. I swung off my saddle and pushed the bike next to me, implying I came in peace. They were certain to have heard what happened to us, the *murungu* and his family at their white-walled house over the hill. I wondered if there was a sense of justice being meted out or a feeling of dim satisfaction I'd been put in my place? Or maybe there was stunned disbelief, genuine shock, because though I had recently provoked a fury in them, I'd never felt any genuine bitterness or hatred from anyone here, just the usual begrudging annoyance at a kid playing daring pranks, acting in ignorance of a wider reality.

Closer to the store I searched for signs of those three presences again, two tall, one short, in blue workman's overalls, cartons of beer in their hands. Even though I knew there was this other project in operation, that Mr Zach had tabs on them in some other place, now that I was back in the vicinity I simply didn't believe it at all. I had cut though the pretence of the scheme, even momentarily, and was convinced they were still about, radiating this awful, undisclosed terror.

I slipped round the back of the building discreetly as possible. The rows of presidential posters were still there. I looked to see if there remained any evidence of my treasonous act, a dried water stain hardened round his face that had creased it, made the ink run lighter, the urine bleaching his cheeks and chin a pale white. But with the bit of heavy rain we'd had, all the posters were looking weathered, dog-eared, crisp, tatty, washed out. To my surprise no one had replaced them.

I CHAINED MY BIKE to a study drainpipe and hoped it would still be there later. I stood, blinking into the low angled sun. I should have packed a pair of sunglasses, a cap. There was a grassless field at the back of the stores, a wide rutted stretch of fine red soil through which clumps of beige wild grass and conical ant mounds jutted. The settling sun made the weathered surface shimmer in places, a dull ruddy sheen. At either end were a set of goalposts, iron frames with no netting, painted gloss white but fast rusting black. They looked lopsided. The field was deserted now, but sometimes in the evenings or the weekends groups of the neighbourhood locals came to play friendly *bora bora*. I used to ride down, circle the field, watching. They played pretty rough, heckling often flared up. A constant plume of agitated soil dusted everyone, but there was a cheery communal atmosphere, charged and masculine, which as an onlooker I envied.

I waited behind the bottle store quietly, resting against the brickwork, biding time. When the light grew thinner and the mosquitoes started to dart, I sprayed my ankles and arms. I slipped on my jeans and boots. When some of the patrons at the bottle store greeted me, I waved back. When one offered to sell me cigarettes or buy me alcohol, I declined. I played on my phone, but not much. I kept peering round the sides of the building for signs of that dust-soiled white Mazda. Occasionally butterflies flared in my stomach, but I took deep breaths, trying to settle them. There was a burning sensation on my thigh. I cupped my hand over the deep wound, pressing down hard, pretending I was being compressed into that slice of skin, that I was a concentration of the pain, nothing but a potent energy force sizing through me.

WE WERE NOW DRIVING down Second Street, then inching up Cork Road. Mr Zach hadn't said very much to me. Even when he was very late, much later than we agreed on, he didn't offer an apology or explanation. I simply got in, off we went. I held onto my satchel, nesting it on my lap, thinking at any minute if my nerves went dead cold I could fling open the door at a traffic light, make a dash into oblivion. I sat watching everything roll towards me, somewhat disbelieving. The roads were dark on the way into town, the oncoming traffic blinding. Everything slow and hazy. We turned left onto Prince Edward Street by the Kensington Shopping Centre and headed towards the concrete rabble of the city centre. I was aware of leaving the safe haven of the suburbs behind.

The intersection of Prince Edward and Samora Machel was chaotic, the traffic lights off. Vehicles jammed in from all sides, the streets were abuzz with pedestrians, scruffy druggie street kids, vendors harassing us. Mr Zach was an impatient driver, his hand pressed constantly to the hooter. Several times this sloven battery of traffic closed in on us from both sides, but he shunted his way through, swearing loudly out the window. We pulled into a stretch of vacant parking on Rotten Row as a huge lorry came lumbering from behind, its great iron weight shuddering through the Mazda, its two stark headlights washing over us in the cab. I sat back and realised how hard I was breathing.

Mr Zach opened his door.

'I will be back soon. Wait here,' he said.

'How long?'

'There are things I need to put in place first. I am coming. Just wait.'

A dull swarm inched past but it was quiet inside the car with the windows up. I calmed myself. There was an avenue of large jacaranda trees stumped along the pavement. Their gnarled bark and knotted branches formed hooded canopies that skewered my vision, filtering everything into sketchiness. The street lights didn't work, their grimy poles stripped of their fittings, and beyond the pavement was the solid sheer wall of a high-rise building which soared upwards without end. A dull chrome-yellowness sunk everything and it took me a while to realise there was yet another riot of election posters pasting the President's face over almost every available surface, crammed into crevices, convexed around street posts and tree trunks. It all looked brash, excessive, signalling this crazed desperation.

Figures, I thought.

LATER MR ZACH STAGGERED BACK, this time with a boozy breath, but he spoke with clarity. We pulled out, carrying on down Rotten Row. It was now I noticed he was wearing a long beige trench coat, buttoned up to his collar and he had dropped a bloated black binliner on the back seat. His clenched jaw made him look severe, staring intently out at the dark, the dense column of road. It was quieter now. We passed the outline of the municipal library, the museum, the College of Music, and in the distance the squat bulk of the Rainbow Towers hotel with its facade of stout fake-gold glass, cheapened by floodlights.

This was where my knowledge of the city ended. We circled an overpass and descended into a wide dual carriageway. We carried on past sprawling warehouses of steel, brick, corrugated roofing. A couple belched black smoke, most lay brooding in darkness. There was a cemetery on the left, overgrown with grass and weeds, crudely exposed to the road, out of place amongst all that industry. We crossed a railway line, turned right, carried onwards.

The warehouses and factories thinned out to tracts of open land, covered in places with scruffy tufts of colourless vlei grass. Most of them were dust bowls with a scattering of dumped litter, the odd carcass of a car or a minibus. A wafer thin mongrel trotted along the roadside, panting and agitated, its eyes slate black in our headlights.

At last there was a large rusted street sign which said, 'WELCOME TO HIGHFIELD'. Mr Zach began to liven up. He made a phone call, speaking in Shona. He sat forward, scanning the area, left and right.

'Are we there?' I asked.

'We are close,' he said.

'Where's the station?'

'Station? What are you talking about?'

'The police station? Where you have my *tsotsis*.'

He let out a short chortle. 'How do you think things are done, out here? Hey, tell me that?'

'I don't understand.'

'Don't worry. You will understand. But there is no station.'

WE WENT DOWN A FEW SIDE ROADS, deeper into this shanty town maze, clawing along. The plots were small and square. Everything looked the same and disorientated me, a sense of dizziness and nausea inching up, honed to fear. The older houses were tiny, made of red-faced brick, built right up against rickety prefab walls. In every spare bit of ground shacks had been erected, wooden or tin, or an extension of plastic sheeting or tarp had been knocked up. There wasn't a blade of grass. It all floated, each block a massive cluttered barge on a sea of fine ochre soil.

A few naked bulbs shone from the *stoeps* of the houses, and I was amazed to think they even had such a thing as electricity out here. But it just dispersed this dull, squalid flush and I felt queasy sifting past it all. There were not many cars about on the roads. I don't recall seeing many people.

We took the next left and stopped by the second house on the right. It was no different from any other.

'Wait here until I call you.'

'What is this place? Why are we here?' I asked.

'Just wait here. I'll fetch you soon and then you will see. Now, you have my money *murungu*?'

'I have it,' I said without pause. 'But I want to know what's going on first.'

'That's fine. You will.'

I nodded. He climbed out and moved towards a property a short way down the road, the bin liner slung over his shoulder. He stopped beside a low prefab wall. On signal two indistinct men emerged out of the shadows, each clasping thick truncheons, maybe even aluminium baseball bats. He tossed them the bag and they moved off towards the house with little hesitation. Mr Zach hung back, pacing up and down. He reached in the pocket of his coat, lifted a cigarette from a box and lit it. Wisps of smoke rose and died in the darkness.

I couldn't hear any commotion, but after a few minutes he flicked the cigarette into a small ditch and strode inside the house. He was walking tall, from behind he looked puffed up. He wore beige leather boots, they crunched the ground beneath him, a crisp punchy step, articulating right then just who Zachariah Singano really was. That sound was unbearable, each step he took was an amplified movement towards some action or event I somehow knew now was terrible and unthinkable, yet couldn't be undone. I sat and waited. Nothing happened for a few moments. It was quiet out on the street where I was. Then he reappeared.

'We have your motherfuckers,' he shouted. 'It's them. Come and see.'

I WALKED ACROSS THE ROAD, or found myself walking, then up these three short steps of polished red stone. Despite knowing something was very wrong, that the plan was deviating from my expectations, I still felt compelled to keep moving. I passed into a small front room brightly lit with a bare bulb where I began to absorb the confusion of the scene. But the moment I caught sight of those three men cowering on the floor I knew right away it wasn't them. It wasn't. Something in me quickly gave way, at the basest level, and in an instant I knew the pretence was finally over. All that hope, that improbable longing. It all flushed out of me in a cold second. And now I knew.

What was I thinking?

They had them pinned there to the ground, in the corner. One of the thugs had his phone out filming Zachariah and his cohort beating these men repeatedly with the truncheons, the flashy bats. They were crying out, slumped and bunched, their arms branched in defensive attitudes, but it was hopeless. They were pinned, writhing there under this onslaught of violence. Zachariah and his men were too strong, the attack had come as too much of a surprise. I could hear sickening thumps to their flesh, the dull thwack against their skulls. They were trying to protest, but it was pointless.

I keeled back towards the door, my stomach clenching, but I was paralysed too. I was standing there watching these three arbitrary men get beaten to a pulp, everything unspooling around me, and I just felt empty and angry and sick.

Zachariah Singano was walking about them, his trench coat now dangling open, his crisp white T-shirt with its brash yellow, green and black screed raging with violent

214

energy under the stark light. He issued the odd numbing kick to the groin and he was almost wailing with glee.

'See,' he shouted, taking the phone from his man and holding it up to me. 'I told you I find your *tsotsis*, no? I find the fuckers and I bring justice. See? Mr Zach he knows. He knows about justice. I told you I can deliver. I told you I can get your three men in blue. Now tell the camera how it feels to get your revenge.'

I then realised he had them all wearing blue overalls. Brand new, just unfolded dark blue overalls, brought out from the bin bag. He knew it was the all-important touch. He knew it was what I wanted, needed to see. It was unbelievable, how he'd forced these three men, whoever they were, to wear those blue overalls and now he was beating the living daylights out of them and all for my show, my gratification. And amidst the bludgeoning and breaking of bones he was letting out wails of delight, these hysterical screams of savage laughter.

I BACKED AWAY TO THE CAR, snatching at the passenger seat for my satchel, then ran down the cramped street fast as I could. I heard those cries and pleas wavering in my ears. Zachariah was screaming at me wildly from the *stoep* as I sprinted off. Glancing back in the blur of speed and panic, I thought I saw the frame of a lean-coated figure lurching down the road after me, but I doubt it. He had made his perverse point, or had wanted to teach me a twisted brutal lesson in my naïve quest for justice. In those last horrific seconds I saw him, the ferocity of his actions seemed motivated by more than the money. I don't even know if he was aware of me being there anymore.

I jogged round this warren for some time trying to navigate my way back to a main road. This limitless energy to keep running came from somewhere, even though my eyes were blotted and I was becoming more breathless, shaking from the inside. Then I stopped, stumbled a few feet towards a ditch, leaned over spewing a blinding force of bitter disgust at the gravelled light red soil. The vomit spattered at the ground like fierce storm fall. I stood up, wiped my mouth, sweat dripping from me. Everything was distorted, the air still and hard against my face, and beneath the jeans my legs burned sharply with pain.

I walked about without direction. There were no people, no figures ambling along the roads, or bodies behind thin curtains in those lighted rooms I passed house by house. Everyone had seemingly slunk away, withdrawn after that Mazda had made an appearance, probably a sign they all knew to watch for, some ominous code. I spent ages moving about in these square circles, fearing I'd end up back at the top of the road where the car was parked, where the house I'd been inside stood in a neat line of others, small and nondescript. I envisioned Zachariah leaning against the cab, smoking a cigarette after his exertions, his two henchmen dealing with the last business of the night, whatever atrocities that included, whatever inconveniences had to be seen to. As I roved about I was scared they might sight me and come after me, prey they could afford to toy with, let loose for a while, before reeling in with easy precision.

I never saw him or his two men again. I don't know what that whole theatre of cruelty, elaborately staged with those blue overalls, was really about. Or who those three poor men were, what dire miscalculation they had made to be cast as the victims in that savage performance. I'm certain there was more to it than merely indulging the base naivety of a desperate boy. I'm sure Zachariah Singano never worked for Special Branch, or at least not in the way

I thought he did. I imagine there wasn't a single scrap of legitimate paper in that folder he waved to get my hopes up. I had fed him all the information needed to bait me. So it was all a depiction, a parade, drawing me in. Somehow I sensed I'd been ensnared into the mechanics of a larger scheme, the dark underbelly of the system, the vile narrative of politics. Its ramifications were too oblique and too distant for me to comprehend then beyond the reviled face of that figurehead printed on the T-shirt he wore under that long trench coat, so potently providing a motivation for everything.

Eventually I spotted this sedate string of lights blinking in the distance, at the tunnelled end of a road I turned into. I scrambled up the grassless incline of a steep ditch and stood there on the main road, half-bent over on the gravel kerb, spitting and swallowing against the dry sourness in my mouth, squinting into the ebbing bright flood of oncoming headlights. I felt vulnerable and conspicuous there, aware that I cast an odd sight, a pale peculiarity against the late press of midnight black. I looked back down over those compressed brooding plains of that township, stunned with some vague terror it would haunt me for a long time to come.

I THUMBED A LIFT FROM HIGHFIELD. A black man stopped on the side of the main road, puzzled to see me all the way out there late on a Friday night. I told him our car had broken down, my father was attending to it, but I needed to get back to the suburbs. He never questioned the logic of this, but invitingly opened the passenger door, sweeping some newspapers and a bowler hat aside for me. There was a mountain of soiled potatoes in the back of his old faded green Datsun truck. The shocks had gone, each pothole we hit rebounded through my spine, agitating my distress, but I was relieved too. The potatoes smelled earthy, a warm comfort, and he told me he was driving from his smallholding out near Lake Chivero to the farmer's co-operative where he hoped to be one of the first in line in the morning to sell his produce. He talked to me for a while, his English broken but intelligible, telling me about his hopes for a good rainy season, to be blessed by his Lord and Saviour. In between he hummed some traditional tunes, chewing sweet smelling tobacco between yellowing teeth. He offered me some sugar beans crammed in an old margarine tub. I felt safe, my uneasiness dissipating the more we slogged through town, then towards the expanses of the suburbs. I offered him some money when we reached the bottle store, but he declined. My bike was still there. I sat out the night, riding over the hill in the morning.

3

DAD GETS A CALL. It's about ten-thirty. When it's an incident of a serious nature, a code one, armed robbery, the call desk alerts him as he feels an obligation as managing director to follow the rapid response team out to the scene. He comes into the study where I've been tapping away at these recollections on my laptop. There is this rigidity cast through his body, this nervous urgency. He's donned a black cap with 'WALKER SEC' embroidered with thick gold thread, the same logo that's on the pocket of the jacket he's busy zipping up.

'Dan, you want to come out on a call?' he asks.

'Sure,' I say.

Mom's asleep. We arm the house remotely as we head out the front door, towards the Hilux which also now has the logo spray-painted on the doors and underneath the company's slogan, 'Don't Let it Happen to You'.

We hop in and swing out onto the driveway, opening the electric gate. Dad drives at some pace, a GPS system guiding us, but the roads are quiet this time of night. He has hands-free systems in the cab that he speaks to his team through every couple of minutes, asking for an update. After having his fingers burnt with Walker Enterprises, Dad set up this new business specialising in bespoke security systems and rapid response units.

We wind through some small roads, finally arriving at a large property, the Walker Sec response truck parked outside, its emergency lights flashing blue, washing the high white walls with this dull rhythmic splurge. Something about it tenses me all of a sudden, and I feel Dad inhale beside me.

He's greeted by one of his staff and quickly briefed. They disappear together in this battery of resolve. I hang back, waiting in the Hilux, not wanting to insensitively invade someone's space in the aftermath of their ordeal. I wonder what has happened here, what manner of violation? I wonder how they scaled the wall or what means of access they used, how they broke in, how they handled the dogs, how they held this home's inhabitants in the grip of their malign intentions? I wonder if anything else, God forbid, occurred other than a mere robbery of replaceable items or cash at the behest of a gun or weapon of some description?

While I'm waiting something of a small restive but timid crowd starts to gather at the gates of the property. Word has quickly spread that something has disturbed the surface gloss of quaint suburbia, the flat ordinariness of existence. In the gathering there are one or two men, even at this time of night, clad in the general commonality of blue workman's overalls, but I don't baulk now at every man in blue. I've realised how dangerous an ambiguity is, that you can look at one man and simply see a figure in blue, just as I made the mistake of seeing a black man through a keyhole and thinking all black men were him.

Eventually Dad gestures to me that it's okay, there's no harm in me coming inside. I leave the truck, slipping on a spare Walker Sec jacket. I enter into the property and walk up the drive way. There is a sense of ease and quiet, no dogs, no hysterical domestic staff, no dimming reverberations of what has occurred.

There's some evidence of household goods which have been ransacked, photo frames splayed on the carpet, a collection of DVD's brushed off a counter, odd ornaments chucked about. In the dining room Dad is sitting with a black couple who must be in their early forties, stiff and shaken, but neither crying nor emotional, just drawn looking, disbelieving.

'It just happened so fast,' the man is saying. 'They were in the bedrooms in no time at all, we couldn't even react.'

Now begins Dad's real task. What's happened can't be unlived or undone and there is no human alive who won't be traumatised or feel the graveness of life's vulnerabilities, but Dad sits with them, takes one of their hands in each of his and begins to talk, just to talk. He's remarkably good at this process, it turns out, knowing how to speak to people who've had frightening experiences, he has a knack, he knows how to talk them through it, to tell them not to worry, to say that everything's going to be all right, that it's all over now.

I've heard him with clients before, just as I'm hearing him again. He's somehow so soothing, so genuine, as if another persona has inhabited him altogether, ingrained and rapt with this sagely, otherworldly wisdom. It's such a contrast I wonder whether it's really true. It seems impossible that when he speaks to all these people in the aftermath of their ordeals, he's ever able to mean a single word of what he says. How can he believe the assurances he utters? I mean it's never all right, is it? It's never going to be over, not really. Maybe in the physical sense, yes, not otherwise. He just believes it needs to be said anyway, that in the absence of truth, comfort is a good counsellor.

There's a small boy in the lounge, not more than five or six. He's sucking his thumb and shaking. Silent tears blot his eyes. An older lady is comforting him, maybe a summoned grandmother, maybe an old *ambuya* house maid, perhaps a matronly neighbour. She has his head to her bosom.

'There, there,' clutching him closer. '*Iye zvino zvino, usatya mwanangu, vaenda saka havachakukuvadze.*'

I bend down and want to place a hand on the boy's shoulder, but I also don't want to frighten him.

'Are you alright young man?' I ask instead.

223

THERE IS THIS WHOLE PROCESS to go through and Dad is nothing if not meticulous. Finally, with everything secured and security men stationed in the house and outside, we depart. Dad doesn't say anything to me on the way back, but sitting next to him I feel this sense of pride, thinking what he does now, the reasons that motivate him, even if it's tough, a fright one never gets used to. All he wants to do is halt the lurking threat which looms out of every dusk fall and dark night. He wants to make people safer, all people, against a simple moral abdication. It's a mighty achievement in my books.

He approaches No. 11 Alice Smith in a slow dead crawl, putting his headlights on full bright, looking up and down the bare wall twice. We stop outside our gate, he glares into the rear view mirror at the dark splurging shadows of Travis Bell's pavement behind us. His eyes move from left to right, his cautious brain processing the visuals, interpreting the data, and only when he's fully satisfied does he press the remote to open our gate. As we inch in I can see him go physically rigid again, gripping the baseball bat that lies beside the seat, his knuckles clenched round its handle tight as a vice. Each and every time we arrive home he follows this ritual, permitting himself no change.

NOW THAT WE'RE BACK I say goodnight to Dad. He treads down the passage and disappears silently into the room where my mother may lie sleeping and closes the door. I grab a bottle of cold water from the kitchen and stand briefly in the doorway of Becca's old room, sipping it. It's dark, but I can see the outline of furniture from the spill of the passage light. Her double bed stands in the middle of the room, opposite the window, the brass bars rising with a cold sheen, the crisp white bedspread seeming to levitate like a slab of lightless marble. I take a few paces in to run my fingers over it. It's cool and soft, the luxuriant feel of clean cotton. The pillows are pouted. I run my hand over her bed again, noticing how meticulously it's been laid out, pressed over with two flat palms.

In my own room, alone now in this private incubation, I permit some of the old doubts, the blame, the cold hard pang of past unalterable fact to come pressing in about me. I'm staring long and hard at the cupboard doors, their white enamelled sheen shining like a monolith in the dull wash of the floodlit garden, knowing all too well what dark sharp secrets of my youth lie hidden there, drawn to them compulsively. It's hard to resist an old addiction, what lies and lives in the gut.

I stagger towards these doors and pull them open. It stands ajar, a screen against the dappled curtained window, blocking the light, and inside the cupboard lies a stack of darkness. I prod about towards the back of the top shelf, my hand delving under the mound of clothing, my fingers feeling for the flintiness of the parcel I once buried here. I touch the shape of the space which held those sharp shards of glass. I can feel them and remember their shapes with intimate precision, as if they're still here, my packet of weapons, and any moment now I could withdraw that glossed smoothness, those curved edges pulsing, a dim ring of mystic light, and run my fingers over their lithic coolness.

I stumble towards my restless bed, aware, almost immediately, as is often the case with these near autistic states into which I veer and levitate, that I have very little clear recollection of what has just taken place. I run my fingers slowly across the ladder of rutted scars on both my thighs, and though my eyes droop over the sway of confusion, and sleep is close, I begin to read those wounds all over again, compulsive as ever, even if the edges are softening, the braided skin, like memory, now softening, but still I read them as if I were a blind man reading braille.

I FREEZE WHEN THE GATE BELL RINGS, fork midway to my mouth. I've been expecting it, the report of the sound shuffling through me, my mind stumbling, almost causing me to drop my fork, the heavy ironstone clang on the plate a predestined belling in my ears.

And Becca's dress is very short, black, satiny, stylish. I scan her in the mirror, a gormless imp in a half-stare, a sinful, secretive brotherly eye-grope, my father's flight down the passage, his censoring tones fading in my ears, his disapproval directed at me. I'll always recall that dress with a mixture of fondness and sadness and horror.

Quite late I fall onto my bed, an inch from deep sleep. I hear the muted sounds of locking up, the distant tinker of empty glasses and plates, the flattening joy of hearing the dogs being given their night-time biscuits. I succumb to this state of carefree abandonment, a child cocooned in a child's cocooning world, order and warmth of a kind that isn't so stifling on such a hot night, but it's the last time I will ever remember feeling like this.

It's happening. A stifled scream somewhere, I'm sitting up in bed, fighting for breath, this fuzzy spectre of dark. Up and down the passage people move, bodies come and go. The odd brief commotion, an escalation of tension. I hear muffled speaking, heavily accented voices, deep and deadpan, curt answers to drawn pleas. There's a dreadful power levitating out there, blanking us, breaking over us.

And it's only a momentary flash of a blue-cladded figure through the keyhole, but the image will linger ingrained in me, imprinted on my brain, fused solid with my nerves, propelling everything I do.

They have gone. The gate slammed open on its coaster. A last sharp exclamation mark closing this long, sinuous paragraph.

It's over, but it's starting.

Breathe.

Try to breathe.

Be brave young Daniel.

You're just a boy, fight for your innocence, fight for it.

Feel the wrapt tension deflate, drain away into this dimming aftermath, this corridor of quietness, flights abreast a white ceiling.

You assume these incidents are a blare of screams and rants, but there was only a purl of murmurs, a tremble of undercurrents. It started with a scream and ended with a slam, but that was not the whole story, not the whole story at all.

Now it's a blur, the next day is something of a blur too, a hot distorted tunnel of time, but the heatwave finally breaks late in the afternoon, the clouds louring in low, the rain starting to fall in an instance of wonder, heavier, harder, intensifying until there's a pelting shower. No one remarks in the wonder of this gift, the respite from the onslaught of the cruel summer sun, the shock it's scorched us with. Only I run out, energised by ignorance and aimlessness, and for the sake of my fast-fading childhood, I force myself to dance a small improvised jig in the runny puddles, skid and slip over the wet spongy lawn.

THERE ARE OTHER PEOPLE'S STORIES which arc out of this sad series of events that I haven't really begun to contemplate or weigh up my responsibility for. With the years that have passed and the old President now finally gone from power, I occasionally visualise a return to Highfield, feeling compelled to go there and make some unknowable, undefinable gesture, even if it's just a sense of enacting some sort of attempt at closure to the whole affair. It's strange, disconcerting, but something still draws my conscience there. I imagine being able to sense its presence as I near, having crossed the sloven dispassion of the city centre and outwards to the townships, where that same sceptic air hovers pervasively and stagnantly. I don't know when or even if a trip will be feasible, or what I really hope to achieve by going, but I can see myself drifting along its disintegrating roads, passing the tiny dilapidated houses, the tatty makeshift shelters. Over everything there will probably be that grey sheen of shanty grime, the sorry pallor of the poor. I will most likely be confused again, by the sameness of every road, the civil squareness of every block. I remember this hazy dullness as if it were most distinct and I feel myself searching for that elusive red brick house with the small *stoep*, the cracked webbed windows, but there will most likely be nothing but a lined score of indistinguishable possibilities. It will be futile, pointless. The decaying legacy of a dead empire ghosts my mind, drives my actions, informs my dreadful conceit, and yet I see myself there, a lone standout figure absorbing the quizzical hostility of the residents, wanting to somehow reach out, make a connection, lay to rest our bitter entwined pasts. I walk and of any frameless face willing to entertain my presence I'm about to risk my delicate acceptance to ask a rather blunt, pointed question. I have a sense what this

228

question will be, opening up a whole other chapter in my attempt to seek atonement, but so far its exact shape and dynamics remain undetermined. I should do it, I should go. But it's equally possible, with nothing ultimately to gain, no entry into knowing, no way of changing the past, I may not go back to Highfield at all.

ACKNOWLEDGEMENTS

I am once again indebted to late Mrs Drue Heinz and the committee of the Hawthornden Fellowship for the gift of a residency in 2015, which allowed for the writing of this novel. Thanks also to Hamish Robinson and his fantastic staff at the castle for making this retreat so hospitable and rewarding for writers.

I am grateful for the advice, support and patience of my literary agent, Veronique Baxter, and everyone at David Higham Associates, London.

For their invaluable input and encouragement over the past six years during the various stages of writing this novel, I extend my heartfelt thanks to Bruce Hunter, Ellah Wakatama Allfrey and Richard Cottan.

Finally, for having the courage and conviction to take this novel on and for his dedication to the craft of producing books of real quality, I extend my sincere appreciation to my editor and publisher, Andrew Latimer, and his team at Little Island Press.

ABOUT THE AUTHOR

Ian Holding's critically acclaimed debut novel, *Unfeeling*, was published in 2005, shortlisted for the Dylan Thomas Prize in 2006 and named a Best Book of the Year by the *Globe* and *Mail* newspaper. This was followed by *Of Beasts and Beings* in 2010. He has twice been a Fellow of the Hawthornden Literary Institute and holds a PhD from the University of the Witwatersrand.